THE BURDEN

KASSIE STRINGER

Copyright © 2019

ISBN: 9781091483033
ISBN-13: 978-1-09-148303-3
Independently Published

To the victims who weren't believed,
And those yet to find the courage to speak up.

Prologue

Bleep...

Bleep...

Bleep...

Bleep...

The monotonous electronic rhythm faded into Anna Miller's ears. A confusing repetition and an unfamiliar one. Unrehearsed in their timing, distant voices, soft footsteps, shuffling papers and the sound of curtains being drawn formed a quiet clinical cacophony, that without sight Anna struggled to distinguish. Beside her, the steady ECG print gained peaks; a change only a trained eye could detect, whilst she was unable to respond in any physical or verbal capacity. She was yearning to move, to switch off the incessant beeping. Despite the will she possessed to do it, everything but her mind remained paralysed.

Aside from the constant and unstoppable beeping of machinery, the only other thoughts ailing her were the recurring flashbacks. She was reliving the trauma that put her in this position.

'Any response yet?' a near, direct female voice asked, bringing Anna's attention immediately back into the room. It was a voice she didn't recognise. If she'd known where she was and what was happening, she'd have been able to make the educated guess that it was a nurse. However, that would have been incorrect.

'No... d'you think she'll pull through?' a second, this time male, voice pierced her ears. Yet another voice she did not know. The first unfamiliar replied instantly.

'I hope so Hayes; she's our prime suspect now.'

The Woman

Collecting her few belongings into a small bag, the five-foot-six journalist was ready to go home. It was Wednesday. She still had more of the working week to struggle through, so was eager to get some rest after the day she'd had, in hope of being ready to face it all again the next morning.

Everything had gone wrong, right from the get go. To start with, the alarm on her smartphone hadn't gone off – perhaps she hadn't set it correctly – so she'd woken up late. Not an ideal start for a young professional who commuted into London every day from a suburb. Leaving the house swiftly, in a rush to catch her train on time, she'd forgotten her coat. It was not only freezing that October morning but raining. Securing yet more misfortune, roadworks had caused chaos for the traffic. Subsequently, the train was pulling away from the station as she ran onto the platform. She couldn't believe it. She huffed, annoyed, but there was nothing she could do. The circumstances were beyond her control. She had to wait the thirty minutes in the bitterly cold drizzle for the next scheduled train. Not that it mattered anymore; she would inevitably be late to work.

By time she had finally arrived at the office, she was stressed. Her accidental failure to comply with the unnatural and obsessive adherence to strict schedules, laid out by corporate moguls, had made her feel inadequate. What's more, her hair was a dripping mess and her floral dress was soaked through to her skin. Worst of all, and as fate would so cruelly have it, she was late on the day the "big boss" had decided to make a rare appearance. Of course, they noticed and looked upon her in disgrace. This low-level journalist would later be scolded directly by her line manager for her tardiness.

It didn't matter that she'd acquired a ridiculous amount of debt, nor that she'd suffered through unpaid work experiences, or even that she'd worked over fifty hours a week to build up her profile enough to secure the position that she was in now. No. All that mattered to the corporate bosses of the capital was that you looked good, you showed up on time and you sat at your desk for eight hours a day – or more if you wanted to be considered good at your job.

'We're goin' for a drink down at Zero, you in?' a tall, skinny colleague with flowing brown hair asked, stepping into her path as she was heading to leave.

'Oh…Uh…'

'Come on. I know you could use a drink,' the colleague pressed her, somewhat unnecessarily. It didn't take much to convince her. Quite honestly, she *could* use the drink.

'Yeah, alright. I'm in,' she smiled and followed her colleague to the small group of similarly dressed women that had formed at the lift.

The Emergency

On the morning of the twenty-fifth of October, at seven fifty-one a.m., the phone rang in the call centre. An operative picked up, answering this frantic call to the emergency services by a Mrs Elizabeth Warren. Immediately, the operative sent paramedics, who rushed by blue-light ambulance to the given address: a large Georgian townhouse bearing long panelled windows, with a bricked upper level and a ground floor cased in a smooth white stone. Protruding from the front was a large stepped entrance leading to a black door and a polished number twenty-nine glinting above a small, paint-covered knocker.

It was a quiet, expensive area. The kind where the properties were ones that only those on a significantly high salary could comfortably afford. A safe, gated neighbourhood where little to nothing went wrong and everyone kept to themselves as they left early each morning in their grey and black suits, getting into their equally bland and equally expensive cars and heading off to their apparently important jobs. Simple small talk may be exchanged between residents over local gossip or perhaps the latest charity gala, but little else. Nothing but suitably forced interactions between those wanting to get back to their own egocentric lives.

A desirable and yearned for life, everyone local knew the area and the types that lived there. With this knowledge instilled into his mind since early adolescence, when he'd been a harmless nuisance with his mates from the estate, local man and ambulance driver Mike instinctively knew that, with no immediate parking on the restrictive street outside, he could pull round the back of the row of houses where there was much easier access. Parking up and quickly grabbing gear from the back, he and fellow paramedic Rachael rushed into the property.

Inside the house, a bleak, modernist style echoed throughout. If it wasn't pristinely cleaned gadgets as the focal point of a room, it would be expensive art or sculptures. They were the pretentious kind of belongings that, if asked, the owners would brag were produced by some artist known only to a niche few.

Of course, carpets were far too high-maintenance for these residents. Instead, beautifully maintained floorboards hid under antique rugs. High ceilings added to the style, with (although the owners may not admit it) fake chandeliers of sorts dropping from them with prominence. The small bursts of colour found throughout convened in fierce contrast to the bland minimalism, immediately distracting the eyes of any who entered. It was, without doubt, the perfect show home.

'Thank goodness you're here, it's through there, I don't know what happened, I came home to find them like that!' The paramedics were met by the near hysterical directions of the caller.

Elizabeth was a small, thin woman with blonde hair casually turning silver. She was soft in the face, and natural ageing was being kind to her, although it was hard to tell for anyone who looked at her in her current state. Her usually expertly done hair appeared unkempt, an out of character untucked blouse hung around her hips, smudged mascara shadowed her eyes, subtle wrinkles appeared each time she found herself unable to keep composure and her normally sparkling blue eyes were struck with a shocked grey.

She led the paramedics down the stairs and through the corridor to a converted bedroom on the lower floor. Regardless of the information they were given before arriving and no matter how much training they'd had, the scene that met the two young responders was an unsettling sight.

Across the room, in a corner between a tall, standing lamp that had been knocked and a desk, was the awkwardly wedged body of a large, middle-aged Caucasian man, with one arm twisted unnaturally against the wall and his head drooping heavily towards the floor. A drying matte of blood was soaking into the floorboards below him. Beneath his blazer, a once paper white shirt had turned a murderous red. Visible to the paramedics were clear and deep lacerations in his stomach and chest. It was the kind that resulted from the thick heavy blows of a large pronged object.

Blood was smeared along the wall next to him, leading to, or possibly away from the bed. Although clearly disrupted, the space around this man identified no immediate weapon or cause of his injuries. One might suggest potential from the few fragments of shattered glass, that laid scattered on the floor before him, but they were evidently too small for the type of wounds the man had suffered, and the shards remained innocently transparent. Originally, it had been a small vase perhaps.

The desk appeared mostly untouched, just a dim inactive monitor still on in the background, with a small humming from the hard-drive next to it. A short USB cable was protruding from the back and resting to the side of the computer. The nightstand between the man in the corner and the bed had a few knocked over or misplaced objects, including a digital alarm clock floating down the front, hanging loosely by its black cord and yet somehow still showing the correct time at eight twenty-three a.m.

On the double bed, ruined Indian-cotton sheets were topped with two equally limp bodies. One a young female, estimated in her mid-twenties, with her head and right arm dangling sloppily off the bed, slow red droplets still dribbling down her arm and gravity assuring her bloodied hair covered her paling face. Not too far from her arm, a hammer rested conspicuously on the floorboards.

Atop the girl, another middle-aged man was slumped almost stiffly over her body, his head resting unconsciously in the nape of her neck. With his back to them, the paramedics could not see any obvious injuries on him and the burgundy sheets on the bed made it difficult for them to instantly assess potential blood loss.

Within almost timeless seconds, they'd taken in the scene. The three practically lifeless bodies that scattered the room were all presumed dead at first sight. What had happened between the three of them in this room was not altogether clear and something neither paramedic wished to try and imagine. They, after all, had to go to bed that night in the safety of their own homes just the same.

After his initial assessment as first responder, Mike immediately radioed for further medical help and the police to be dispatched. He looked to his colleague, her eyes reflecting his own shocked and unsettled feelings. Like in every situation they faced, that one brief exchange was all they had time for. Their job was not to get caught up in the emotion or mystery of the events but to simply react to the situation in front of them and focus on the preservation of life. Hard though it may seem to defy their empathetic human nature, any feelings they experienced would be suppressed until they were off duty – perhaps after five or more further callouts to other incidents during their long and arduous shift.

Armoured with latex gloves, they scanned the room, searching for the most immediate danger and most serious injury and got to work. Mike rushed towards the figure in the corner as Rachael approached the bed, both wary of the anxious housewife hovering in the doorway.

'Do you live here ma'am?' Mike asked warmly but directly as he stooped to search for any sign of life in the corner.

'Yeah. Yes. I just got back this morning, and, and, this, are they OK?' Elizabeth answered, collecting her thoughts but plainly desperate to know if these people – presumably her relations – were still breathing.

'Alright, thank you ma'am. And do you know who these people are? What are their names?' Mike smiled reassuringly to her, as he concluded that the first patient was already dead. He gave Rachael a knowing look to transfer his findings inaudibly. Rachael nodded.

'That's my husband.' Elizabeth's response came with a shaking finger indicating which man her husband was. Luckily, thought Mike, she was pointing to the man on the bed, but then as Elizabeth turned to the man in the corner, in attempt to offer his identity, her emotion choked her again and she was unable to speak for a moment. She had realised, the moment Mike had stood, that he was dead. Tears of dread and fear fell uncontrollably from her eyes.

'Thank you, the information you're giving is really helping. Now can you tell me what your husband's name is, please…Elizabeth?' Rachael stepped in as she neared the bed, setting down the kit. Elizabeth nodded.

'It's Joe,' she swallowed. 'Joseph Warren. He's a doctor, uh, cardiologist.'

The name struck both paramedics straight away.

Of course, they now knew who they were dealing with. Doctor J. Warren was one of the most famous doctors in the community. Not only was he one of the leading cardiologists in the country, he was a renowned media personality, with regular spots on morning television and radio talk shows. He did numerous public events and charitable acts, and most recently was in the running to become Head of Cardiology at one of the busiest, research focused hospitals in the Imperial College Healthcare portfolio: Hammersmith – one of the trusts the paramedics themselves worked for.

A hero in scrubs, a charismatic man, a husband, a father and now, potentially and sickeningly, a corpse. Quite suddenly, both paramedics felt an overwhelming sense of additional pressure. It always seemed so much worse when dealing with one of their own.

'And that's Ed Braithwaite, oh, Eddy!' Elizabeth finally managed to get out before tears welled up and bawled out once more, but the dead man was no longer a main concern for the two.

'Thank you,' Rachael smiled sympathetically as she leaned towards the doctor's body. Instantly, she could feel air flowing from his nostrils. Relief spread through her. He was alive. Still. For now.

'Good news Elizabeth; he's still breathing and we're going to do everything now to keep him safe and get him to the hospital as quickly as possible, OK?' Rachael knew it would be reassuring to explain to the patient's understandably shaken wife what was happening but remembered to add the cautious questioning to check that Elizabeth was actually listening. It was very common for people in a state of shock to be unresponsive and foggy, so Rachael was keen to ensure she was taking in what was happening.

A noise escaped the woman. An animalistic exhale of relief that her beloved husband was not dead. Rachael knew that Elizabeth was in no state to be seeing or handling too much more. Just coming home to this, she'd been exposed to more than most could deal with, and she needed to be removed from the situation.

10

'We're waiting on another ambulance and the police to arrive, do you think you will be able to go out and flag them down for us please, whilst we get sorted in here? It would be a huge help,' Rachael asked politely as she began a further assessment of Doctor J. Warren.

Elizabeth nodded and obliged, dabbing the puddles in her eyes with a crumpled tissue she'd taken from her pocket before turning to do as she'd been asked.

'Wait!' Mike called abruptly. 'Sorry, what about her, do you know who she is?' he asked as he held up the hair of the awkwardly positioned female he'd began attending to reveal her face.

Elizabeth focused, perhaps out of her own curiosity. She looked at the smooth features of the young woman. Her thin greying lips were closed tightly below a small nose. Pale, bruising cheeks supported long lashes from her closed eyes, and a bloodied forehead was matted with an equally bloody and messy mop of dyed blonde hair. A puzzled, somewhat disgusted look crossed Elizabeth's face.

'I don't know her,' she replied honestly and left the room, not allowing for any further questions.

Mike, who was crouched down on the floor, let go of the patient's hair and looked up to Rachael, who looked back to him, both clueless to her identity.

'Well, whoever she is, she's still breathing.'

The Call

The shrill tone of a phone ringing caused the sleeping bodies to stir in the bed, but they did not wake. It wasn't as if it was particularly early, but they'd had a late night to say the least.

The phone rang again. Rob, a tall, broad man in his late thirties, groaned and turned over, nudging his companion with his bare arm. She shook him off.

'Abs, it's for you,' he grunted through his sleep.

She reached for her phone clumsily, not overly familiar with the spacing of his bedside cabinet, as he returned to his slumber.

'Yeah?' she mumbled blearily, answering the phone as she sat up, using the sheets to cover her bare legs. She was wearing nothing but underwear and a plain vest top, which she wore under the same plain shirt every day. The caller spoke rapidly. She scratched her head listening.

'When?' she asked suddenly, alarming Rob. He turned, propping himself up on the pillow and rubbing his eyes free from tiredness.

'Text me the address. I'll be right there,' she instructed the caller, scrambling around for her clothes.

'Saved by the bell again?' Rob taunted. She turned to him, buttoning that familiar white shirt, an awkward apologetic smile

12

spreading across her face. He looked to the foot of the bed, shaking his head and snorted a disbelieving chuckle.

'Uh... thanks, for last night... again,' she tried, tucking her shirt into her grey, straight-legged suit trousers and looking around for her shoes.

'Any time Abbie. Apparently, any time.' He mumbled the last part under his breath. Not that it would have mattered if he'd have said it out loud; she wasn't listening to him. She was too busy scuffling around for her shoes, ready to leave.

He was annoyed at himself. He didn't know why he kept going on this self-destructive streak. He liked the woman, but she was giving him nothing. She was always too scared to take the plunge. He should have known better by now, but he just couldn't help himself. He pushed the covers off himself and got up, walking across his apartment in nothing but his boxers. He went into the bathroom. She waited hesitantly.

'I got you a toothbrush.' He reappeared, handing her a travel pack with a toothbrush and small tube of paste. She stared at him, her eyes widening with panic and her teeth grinding in discomfort.

'Uh...' she dithered, looking at the item in his outstretched hand.

'It's toothpaste Abbie, I'm not handing you a key to my place.' He raised his eyebrows, waiting for her to be a rational adult. Hesitantly, she accepted the toothbrush.

'Thanks.' She gave him a small smile. He walked across to the front door and opened it for her.

'Until next time...' he nodded, standing aside for her to pass.

'There won't be a next time,' she lied to herself, walking across the threshold onto the balcony.

'That's what you always say,' he reminded her, with an air of lingering frustration in his tone. 'Now, get lost Detective.'

The Crime Scene

The second ambulance had arrived promptly, and paramedics poured into the bedroom to aid Mike and Rachael with the two unconscious patients, followed closely by the police and crime scene investigation team. Detective Inspector Ellis Hayes was the first plain-clothes detective to enter the busy scene forming inside the bedroom and corridor.

Dressed in the more comfortable blue chinos with a shirt and casual jacket, he was a shorter man at around five-foot-nine, with the beginnings of a rounded stomach that formed after a few years of married bliss. He had trusting chocolate eyes to compliment his clean-cut brown hair and a matching beard that he'd proudly grown and now carefully maintained. He had a wealth of experience in domestic homicide cases under his belt and his seeming informality gifted him an ability to obtain reliable witness statements, often persuading people into giving him information without realising. He was indisputably good at his job, albeit a little too close to the book.

'What's the damage?' he called to Mike, who was finishing injecting Joseph Warren with some transparent liquid that Hayes couldn't name if he tried.

'One dead, corner. Mm, Ed something. He's all yours. These two are unconscious, serious we presume, we're about to free 'em of each other and get them to accident and emergency. We'll be at Charing Cross.'

'Great thanks,' Hayes smiled and walked over to inspect the corpse in the corner. It wasn't a pretty sight, but he'd seen much less dignified and much more horrific deaths than this before.

Blood was still oozing its way out of the body, desperate to escape into the floorboards beneath the body. The size of the crimson pool surrounding him made it hard to believe there was any blood still left inside. Deep blows to the flesh were visible through the stained, torn shirt, his insides open for viewing. The victim's head was sombrely and stiffly bowed. It was undeniably a sorry and brutal loss of life, so Hayes took a brief moment of silence to honour the victim's life before getting on with his job.

Behind the detective, Mike, Rachael and the other paramedics had safely stabilised both patients, ready to move apart and be transported to the nearest emergency department. Starting with Joseph, the team began to lift his tall and oddly placed body from the unidentified female beneath him. As the four paramedics tried to shift the healthy-weighted doctor, they were surprised to find they were met with some resistance. They placed the body down momentarily to regain some strength before coordinating a stronger lift. This time, as they raised him, a faint squelching noise raised alarm amongst them. The paramedic with the least grip on the patient let go to examine the cause.

Unbeknownst to them all, a cold metallic cord was joining the patients, a connection that would impact their lives in unimaginable ways. A pair of large, silver scissors. One blade withdrawing from the flesh of the doctor's stomach. The other half remaining firmly impaled into the bony torso of the woman.

15

Able to see from her position, Rachael announced, somewhat unnecessarily, 'we've got a bleed!'

At the very moment the medics began carefully extracting the rest of the blade from the man in their hands, leaving the other end still thrust into the female's upper pelvis, Hayes' partner, and Senior Investigating Officer on the case, Detective Chief Inspector Abigail Lowe entered the room.

Bent down over the deceased, Hayes looked up to see his partner's authoritative frame, in her standard grey pantsuit, through the gap between the two patients' bodies. For any normal person entering a room covered in blood, whilst a pair of long, sharp scissors were being removed from flesh, the scene would have caused instant disgust, perhaps even retching. Yet, it seemed to have no adverse effect on this thirty-four-year-old.

Lowe was almost entirely unperturbed by the scene around her as she walked across to her partner, who, without question, began placidly describing the area and actions in the room. It was easy, in a way, for the detectives to dehumanise the process because it was simply their job.

'Spoke with the wife before coming in. ID on the vic Edward Braithwaite, injured one Joseph Warren, doctor by profession...and a Jane Doe.' Hayes finished his description of the scene, before they both turned to watch Joseph Warren being carried out on a stretcher to the first ambulance. Lowe caught the eye of one of the junior officers in the room.

'Follow them to the hospital. I want security, police escort on the rooms of these two,' she indicated to the woman on the bed, 'and try and get any personal items to confirm IDs and physical evidence from them. You know the drill. We'll follow you up to take a statement from the wife once we're done here. Try and calm her

16

down if you can. Hysterics aren't helpful for recounting events.' Lowe finished.

The officer agreed, nodding in obedience and followed the medic team out, but not before Lowe added a thank you. Though assertive, she still had manners.

With the first patient on his way to the hospital, Lowe turned her attention to the average frame of the woman on the bed. Her head had been rested back onto the pillows, her dirty blonde hair was conditioned with drying blood from a head injury and a transparent mask covered her face, air being pumped into her by another paramedic.

The rest of her body was sprawled across the bed, twisted at the knee. Scissors stood erect through her clothing on the right side of the hip, surrounded now by thick bandages to stem bleeding. The flowing hem of her loose floral dress was lifted to her stomach on the left, with a pale, freshly bruised limb protruding down towards the detectives. She'd be lucky to survive whatever happened here, thought Lowe, watching as the paramedics began to move this dead-weight of a woman in her unconscious, breathing-assisted state.

Lowe stared, barely blinking, for a long while as the woman was lifted out of the room on an ugly orange board. It was time for her to get to work. She assessed the situation quickly in her brain. Two middle-aged men. A young female. A basement bedroom. A clearly fatal fight. Taking an educated guess, Lowe assumed an attempted sexual assault which had gone horribly wrong for the perpetrators.

However, her job was about more than just guessing. Her job was gathering evidence, statements and investigating subjective memories of the truth until they formed a likely and attestable narrative. It was about proving what happened, and though she would be the last to admit it, Lowe always felt personally responsible

17

for gathering enough solid evidence to bring justice for the victim. It was what made her good at her job.

'Abbie, you alright?' Hayes interrupted her thoughts. She turned to him.

'I'm fine.' She lifted her cheeks to convince him. He coughed awkwardly.

'You've…uh…missed a button there,' he pointed out. Slightly embarrassed, she did the button up, but did not let it bother her. Hayes squinted, assessing her face for answers, but she would give nothing away.

'Right, let's alert the coroner, get forensics and blood spatter in here. I want to know whose blood is where and why. Let's get him bagged up for autopsy once the site team are done. We should get a look around the house too,' she ordered, her mind on nothing but the job in hand.

'Bloody mess if you ask me. He's a personality, this doctor guy, apparently. Media are gonna be all over it, so you know the Super'll be watching us like a hawk,' Hayes commented.

'Shit.' Lowe took out her phone to Google him, aggressively swiping away a text from Rob that he'd already left.

She opened the internet and typed in the doctor's name. She clicked and scanned through various articles, learning quickly that he was a renowned cardiologist, who did a lot for charity, was constantly pictured with his wife and sometimes children and appeared on morning TV and radio. It was a wonder the man ever slept. There seemed to be no negative article written about him.

She thrust her phone back into her pocket. 'Great… looks like a real hero. Can you get the desks to do a background check on the dead vic and send us over the deets? Also see if we can get an ID on the girl asap.'

'Already done.'

Lowe smiled thankfully at her partner, before scanning the room, her trained eye sweeping over every minute detail.

A soft off-white (or what the owner may insist was "eggshell") paint covered the walls and skirting. Fairly fresh. The room, and rest of the property from what she'd gathered upon entering the house, was well-maintained. Perhaps the result of a bored housewife. The basement bedroom seemed an odd addition to the house in her opinion – especially with only tiny windows on the upper wall above the desk. It was a direct contrast to the open, airy feel of the rest of the house.

In the corner near the door, a small, unremarkable wardrobe neighboured a nightstand and the bed in the centre of the room. On the floor in front of it, an old hammer, red at the face and claw, was being photographed and bagged up for evidence, whilst blood swabs were taken from the surrounding area.

'The sheets, I want to know if there are any traces of semen on them.' Lowe's blunt instruction momentarily halted the productivity of the room.

Hayes looked up to her tentatively. There was an element of uncertainty surrounding Lowe altogether since this was only her fifth case as SIO and she wasn't always the easiest to work with. The truth was she was honest, unpredictable, intuitive and intensely private, and these traits often garnered confusion, jealousy and irritation amongst her colleagues – except for Hayes.

He admired her character and knew that, regardless of her nature, she was an incredible detective and, somewhat annoyingly, she was usually always right. He knew she was damn good at her job and her hunches served her well. Together, they were a successful partnership and complimented one another.

Though Hayes would never admit this to his partner, he'd been offered the promotion to "Chief Inspector" first, but with the birth of his second son last year, he had asked their immediate boss Detective Superintendent Mark Tabbot to consider Lowe instead. Firstly, because she deserved it just as much as he did and secondly so that he could alleviate some of his responsibilities to focus on his family. Although Lowe would never admit it either, she knew her partner was the reason she had the position, and she was grateful.

After much deliberation, their superior had finally agreed, so long as Hayes continued on acting as her deputy on all major investigations. Initially Hayes had hoped Lowe getting the promotion would free him up for more "desk-duty", but she'd had his back for so long, that for her to have her shot too, he'd give anything. The only downside was that the team still responded better to him. This was partly down to some deep-rooted sexism, partly Lowe's testy personality.

'Uh, Lowe—' Hayes began, seeing the unsure reactions around the room.

'I want to rule out sexual assault,' she offered, turning sharply towards him.

'Bit early for assumptions. Perhaps let's wait and when the two come around at the hospital, see what they say?' he suggested, looking over the team to ensure they got back to work.

'If,' Lowe corrected him. He turned her away from the workforce and tried to reason with her in hushed tones.

'You can't just jump to that conclusion Abs. We don't know what happened yet. There's no immediate evidence to suggest sexual assault. Let's wait—'

'Ellis, did you see how she was lying? That girl?' Lowe asked under her breath, her deep brown eyes bearing into his.

'Don't overthink it just yet.' He sighed before adding, 'Besides a man like Warren, you don't want to go accusing a respected guy like that too early. It could ruin the man.'

'And the man could have ruined the woman.' Lowe stood firmly, staring at him until he caved.

'OK, bag it up,' he agreed, turning and calling to forensics. After all she was SIO and wanted it sent for analysis. There was no harm in covering the bases. It was a hunch she had and if she was wrong, she was wrong. However, he couldn't risk the chance that she could be right. Testing was the only way to be sure.

'And Hayes, phone them. Get them to do a kit on the girl,' Lowe added. Hayes obliged, taking out his phone and calling the officer en route with the ambulances.

He turned back to Lowe as he waited for an answer. 'We could put a wager on it now if you're so sure...'

'Behave,' she relaxed, smiling and rolling her eyes at him. He'd lost far too many bets to be trying again.

Her warm response lingered as she walked behind him to continue scanning the room. She looked over the desk, handling objects disinterestedly as her fingers trailed across the monitor and keyboard. Curious, she pressed a key. The screen flashed into life.

'Hayes look at this!' Lowe called, a subtle tone of excitement jumping in her voice. He joined her at the screen, phone still to his ear. A clear video editing software was open on the monitor with a pop-up box displaying the statement "Video input ejected: file not found".

'And there's the cable, connects to a camera, right?' She pointed to the USB cable still attached to the computer.

'But no camera...' Hayes suddenly understood her tone, taking the phone away from his ear.

'No camera.'

A lead.

A smile of satisfaction crossed Lowe's lips. They both turned.

'Hey, has anyone seen or bagged up a camera?'

Most of the workers in the room muttered a no or shook their heads. Lowe rushed out of the room, asking teams along the way if they'd seen or picked up a camera. None of them had.

Then the even more frustrating question began to boil in her brain; if they hadn't picked it up, then who had?

Once outside, with no camera in sight, a deflated Lowe looked at the emerging crowd on the street; interested and gossipy neighbours hovered beyond the yellow tape barrier, awaiting any piece of information that would set them ahead of the next person. Local press setting up, ready for comment. Obviously, she'd need a press and community liaison, but right now her mind was not on that. It was on one thing only.

'What now?' Hayes joined his partner outside the house.

'We find that camera.'

The Wife

Elizabeth sat on the end of a row of plastic chairs in a bland empty corridor. Harsh fluorescent lights scowled down from the ceiling, drawing attention to her darkening exhausted features. All she could do in this moment was wait. Everything was out of her hands.

Her husband was in surgery and she had no idea if he was going to survive it. She had no idea what was happening or how serious his injuries were. She'd been given so little information to go on. She wanted to phone her children for some comfort, but even then, she didn't know how to bring herself to tell them, how to find the words. She would have to do it soon. Her husband was a public figure and all those years by his side had taught her that it wouldn't be long until news of this started to appear online, on television and in the papers. She didn't want them to hear the news from some journalist from some media outlet. She needed to be the one to tell them. It had to be her. Yet, there was a part of Elizabeth that was simply still in too much shock.

She was still trying to get her head around what she'd found in Joseph's study. She'd been to the South of France that half-term week and before returning home, she had dropped their two children back at their respective schools (for the start of term). Already a little tired from excessive driving, she was looking forward to getting in, running a nice warm bath and catching up on some sleep.

Never in a million years did she think she'd walk in to find their good family friend Eddy dead, nor her husband bleeding and unconscious whilst slumped over some random girl in the spare bedroom that he had insisted they convert a few years earlier.

It wasn't unusual for the two men to be down there. Joseph had taken to using it as both a home office to catch up on paperwork and a bedroom to sleep in when he'd come in at who-knows-what hour after work, so not to disturb his wife in the middle of the night. Recently, he'd been working on a new research paper with Eddy, so they'd been spending plenty of time in there. It made sense for them to be there. It didn't make sense for whoever that young woman was to be there. Elizabeth hadn't seen her before and had no idea how she came to be there…though she had her suspicions.

Trying to take it all in and calm herself, she silently stared into the deep blue dado rail opposite her. To think that after nearly twenty years of marriage, the father to her two children, who she'd celebrated years' worth of career success with, always supporting his progress whilst she oversaw the building of a beautiful home… all that was now resting in the hands of a team of surgeons.

'Mrs Warren?' Lowe interrupted Elizabeth's memories.

Elizabeth stood up, startled and scanned the detective from bottom to top. The flat, closed shoes designed for comfort over style, the loose legs of the grey pantsuit, the matching suit jacket and boring shirt, that Elizabeth noted seemed to be a bit too tight for her. Her black hair was tied back in an effortless ponytail and two dead eyes, the colour of burnt coffee, were staring back to meet Elizabeth's own.

'Mrs Warren, I'm the Senior Investigating Officer for the incident involving your husband, is it alright if we ask you a few questions?' Lowe indicated subtly to her partner beside her. Elizabeth blinked between them, registering the abrupt words that had disrupted her manic thoughts.

'It's just a few simple questions, to help us start piecing together what happened Mrs Warren. Would you like to come and get some tea or coffee, might be nice to have something to eat and drink?' Hayes, with his open face, smiled reassuringly.

Lowe looked to him annoyed, she wasn't interested in making pleasantries with case witnesses, especially not those married to the potential offender. It was also inefficient to her. She just needed the answers, not new friends.

'Oh, no. Thank you. I don't think I could, not right now.' Elizabeth responded to Lowe's relief.

'I understand Mrs Warren. Is it OK if we ask some questions here?' Hayes continued, signalling for them to sit down on the chairs. She nodded and sat, he beside her. Lowe remained standing opposite them, arms folded across her chest.

'Great, thank you. Now Mrs Warren, can you tell me what you were doing before you came to find your husband Joseph and the other two people in the bedroom?' Hayes began.

'Uh, Elizabeth, please. I, I was in France last week and uh through the weekend. We have a place in St. Tropez. It's just lovely there. Peaceful. I like to go whenever I can.' Elizabeth looked to the detectives hesitantly. As both were listening intently, she continued. 'It was half-term you see, so I'd taken our children out there—'

'How old are your children?' Lowe interrupted.

'Grace, our eldest is nineteen and Theo is fifteen now,' she paused uncertainly, watching Lowe, waiting for some form of follow up question.

'Please, continue,' Lowe instructed simply, not asking anything further about the children. They were probably irrelevant.

'Uhm, OK, when, uh, when we got back, no, well there were some delays and so I had to drop Grace straight back at University. Oh, she is studying so hard, doing medicine like Joe did, she's in her first year. Um, anyway, then I had to drop off Theo, he's at Wellington in Berkshire, it's a, um, boarding… well he stays there during term time. Their education is important to us…'

Elizabeth began to get upset, as the thought of telling her children what had happened struck her again. Lowe rolled her eyes, shifting her weight to her other foot impatiently. Hayes shot her a warning glance whilst giving Elizabeth a supportive pat on the shoulder. As soon as this was over, she would call them. She knew they'd want to know and speaking to them would provide her with some small support or relief. Elizabeth loved her children more than anything.

'Mrs Warren, when did you get back to your house?' Lowe questioned directly, trying to move her along. Elizabeth wiped her wet eyes and thought.

'So, I'd stayed overnight in a hotel, near Theo's school, um after all the driving I was too tired that night so then drove back, um, it must have been around quarter past six this morning I left off. I wake early you see. Always have done since I was about twenty. I got home just before eight I guess. I didn't check the time.

'Uhm, Joe usually does the later shift, so I was expecting him to be home. I was, uhm, looking forward to seeing my husband after a week apart – obviously. He hadn't been able to get the time off to come away with us, they're so understaffed at the hospital these days, you know how it is, plus he's been working on his latest research paper and he's been doing a lot extra because he's looking to become the Head of the Unit or something… Uh, anyway, I called around and he wasn't in the living room, so I thought he would be in his study, which is the downstairs bedroom. He spends a lot of time there and that's when, when, where I found him and Eddy like that…

Oh, I didn't know I'd find him like that.' Elizabeth looked helplessly to Hayes, tears shimmering against her bluey-grey irises.

'It's alright, you're doing really well Elizabeth. We really appreciate it,' Hayes assured her calmly.

'Then what did you do, once you saw them?' Lowe inquired bluntly, unaffected by Elizabeth's display of emotion.

'I didn't know what to do!' Elizabeth cried. 'I, I called an ambulance. It was just instinctive. Then I waited for them to arrive.'

'And when was the last time you'd spoken to your husband?'

'It must have been early yesterday evening. I'd text him to say I'd dropped of the children and was staying overnight. He replied saying he was having Eddy over, to go over the latest draft of his paper and that he'd see me in the morning when I got home. Uhm…I also messaged Eddy, uh, just to make sure that Joe had dinner. The man can tell you anything on a human heart, but he can't cook for himself,' she exhaled thoughtfully. 'Uh, I can show you the texts…'

'Oh, that won't be necessary just at this moment – thank you.' Hayes stopped Elizabeth from twisting to reach inside the pocket of her beige trench coat that was draped over the back of the seat.

It wasn't necessary as they'd be able to confirm through records on both Joseph and Eddy's phones which the team had already collected for evidence. They'd recovered them, along with what they presumed were items belonging to the unknown woman, from a vehicle belonging to Ed Braithwaite which had been parked on the street outside.

'If I'd have known that could be the last time I would speak to him, I would have phoned. If I'd called maybe he'd be OK, maybe we wouldn't be sat here…' Elizabeth settled back into the chair. Hayes tried to comfort her, giving her a much-needed pause in the questioning, as she mused over meaningless what-ifs.

Lowe studied the wife. Something in Elizabeth's sentence seemed weird. Firstly, Lowe couldn't work out who she was more upset about not calling: her husband or her husband's friend? The chronology of her sentence confused Lowe's interpretation. To Lowe, it seemed she was more upset about the friend.

Not only that but Elizabeth had also said it was "instinctive" to call an ambulance and that was the very first thing she did. However, very few people who found their husband, friend or even a stranger unconscious and covered in blood, immediately phoned an ambulance. Instinct would encourage them to run to the person and check whether they were alive or breathing, and then try and help them. They would hold them, check if they were conscious, maybe scream out. Then they'd call for help. Often, people openly expressed that they checked to see if whoever was injured was breathing, possibly to settle their own conscious and heroize themselves in their version of events. Yet, Elizabeth had not.

Lowe thought harder. It seemed especially strange to her that, with the amount of blood at the scene, Elizabeth's light clothing was completely clean. It was unlikely then, that she had even checked to see if they were alive. If she had, there would undoubtedly be blood transferred onto her loose pale blouse – right? Why wouldn't she have checked if any of the three were alive first, or at the very least her husband?

'Have you changed your clothes today?' Lowe bent down suddenly to ask her. Elizabeth looked up to meet Lowe's close, candid gaze. Her reddened eyes narrowed in confusion.

'No? Uh no.' Elizabeth was puzzled. Hayes looked to Lowe, equally perplexed and uncertain of her line of questioning.

'You didn't try and see whether either your husband, Ed Braithwaite, or even this woman you don't know were alive before phoning for an ambulance?' Lowe probed further.

'I, I...' Elizabeth stumbled, unsure on how to respond or why this specific action was even being questioned in the first place. It wasn't weird at all. It had merely been her reaction to the shocking event. Get help. That was her instant thought.

She tried to explain herself: 'They looked dead... and there was so much blood. I just, I just didn't think to. I called nine-nine-nine straight away.'

'Let me just be clear Mrs Warren, you did not touch any of the three people in that room, or make any attempts to see if they were still alive?' Lowe was pushing harder than necessary, and Elizabeth was rapidly transitioning from upset to angry. She certainly did not appreciate the judgmental tone from the detective, even though just moments before, she herself had been judging the detective's appearance. It was different though, judging looks and judging character.

'No,' Elizabeth responded sharply.

'Forgive me, but that doesn't seem right. Most people in your situation would probably want to know if their husband – of twenty years is it? – was still alive...' Lowe stood back up, unable to keep her thoughts to herself.

Elizabeth immediately resented her. Who did this woman think she was? Who was this soulless person picking fault in her reaction to a seriously appalling incident? The detective didn't have any idea what it was like to find people you care about in that position, so who was she to cast judgement?

'DCI Lowe...' Hayes tried to stop her to no avail. Elizabeth stood up too, in no state to take accusations from this trying woman.

'Most people don't come back to find a crime scene in their house. I'm sorry I didn't read the rulebook on how to act when your friend – and husband – are dying right in front of you. But I can tell you this now, I didn't do anything to my husband, or Eddy, or whoever that girl is. Do you have any idea what it's like to come home and find that? No, of course you don't. I came home this morning, and I found them like that, so why don't you, instead of standing here and accusing me, go and find out what happened and do your goddamn job?! Instead of standing here and acting like a know-it-all, why don't–'

'Did you pick up the camera?' Lowe interjected, ignoring practically everything the wife had just said.

'The camera?' Elizabeth stopped mid-sentence and stared at the detective, stunned. Hayes looked between the conflicted women.

'The camera,' Lowe repeated, impatient for an answer.

'What? No. What are you talking about?' Elizabeth looked between the two detectives.

Finally, Lowe stood down, still vexed. She'd really hoped the wife had picked up the camera. It was the only obvious answer for its whereabouts, but clearly Elizabeth had no idea.

'Right, well I'll go and do my goddamn job and find it then.' With that, Lowe walked off down the hospital corridor, without another word.

'Uh, thank you for your time Mrs Warren, Elizabeth. One of our officers will be in touch and when you're ready please come down to the station and give an official statement to help us continue the investigation.' Hayes concluded the discussion awkwardly, Lowe's attitude hanging wearily in his mind. He wasn't sure why she was so forceful and off-track in this conversation; that wasn't like her at all.

He followed after Lowe, leaving a flustered Elizabeth to wait for news on her husband.

The Detective

'What the hell Abbie?! You can't go in like that... we weren't supposed to "good cop, bad cop" it with a spouse. She's probably still in shock! What were you thinking?' Hayes stressed to his partner. There was no reason for her to have acted as she did, and without any compassion at all for the wife.

'I know. I just. It is weird, don't you think, to not check the husband at least?' Lowe huffed. Her logic wasn't wrong.

'I mean, a little,' Hayes admitted, 'but you can't act like that Abs. You can't just pull accusations out of thin air without any cause. C'mon...'

'I didn't accuse her of anything Ellis, it just made me think, maybe she'd gone in there, seen all this and seen the camera, and maybe, just maybe, it might not look good for her husband – or the friend – so she'd hidden it. That's all. Maybe she knows one of them is a bad person. Maybe her relationship with her husband isn't as loving as all these articles make out and that's why she didn't touch him? I think there might be more to her story.'

'Alright, alright. I guess that makes sense. Maybe in future, let me know your train of thought and uh, maybe let me question the wife?' Hayes suggested, somewhat cheekily.

Lowe stopped walking and looked at him unamused.

'What? I mean, c'mon, I don't think she likes you very much…'

'No.' Lowe continued walking. 'I doubt I'm bleached enough for the upper-class wives, or maybe I'm just not manicured enough,' She commented, flicking her nails up sardonically.

Hayes decided it was best to not respond to this. It was not his place. Lowe was a plain, natural woman who generally took little care over her appearance. Not that she necessarily needed to or was unattractive, but there were simply more important things that mattered to her. Her motivations were all inwards.

Like many in the area, Lowe had been raised on a decaying council estate and had known many hardships, which had probably granted her a slight resentment to those with wealth. She'd spent most of her younger years in and out of the care system, after her father abandoned the family and her mother turned to drugs and alcohol. When she was sixteen, with her mother deteriorating into an addicted waste of oxygen, she practically became the sole carer for her younger sister, Shannon.

One day, Lowe had been at her part-time job which she worked nearly every day after school and at weekends to earn money to buy food for the family and meet rent. It was at one of the smaller local supermarkets as a Checkout Assistant that paid minimum wage, but it was all she could manage to find. Jobs were scarce in the area and so she'd taken what she could.

Whilst she was there, aimlessly serving customers as they shopped for their groceries, tragedy was barging into the front door of her home, forcing entry to terrorise the two inside: her mother and her sister. The dealers, to whom her mother owed a great deal of money, had shown up.

At half nine, the young Lowe walked the short distance from the shop back to their flat, staying cautiously under the path of the street lights. It was always a risk, being a lone young girl, walking unaccompanied at night on this estate, but she did it out of necessity again and again every evening.

She arrived at the front door, a hideous burnt red with a broken number eight, and was surprised to see the lights weren't on in the small front room and the door was slightly ajar. Possibly her mother was out looking for another way to ruin their lives again.

Suspecting nothing, Lowe entered, closing the door behind her and taking her shoes off in the small narrow hallway. Turning towards the lounge, she flicked on the light. And then she saw. A whole world of mess, hatred, illegality, comeuppance: murder. On the shaggy torn carpet, her mother's beaten, bruised and bleeding body was scrunched in the corner. Lowe had screamed. Screamed for help. Shouted. Tried to violently shake life back into her murdered mother.

But she was dead. Stone. Cold. Dead.

Frantically, Lowe cried out for Shannon, hoping she'd hidden in a wardrobe and was safe. It was not to be.

On the grimy tiles of the tiny kitchenette, Shannon had been battered into the ground. So innocent at just twelve years old, the dealers had not spared any mercy. Her clothes had been ripped off of her and there were deep stab wounds across her torso, arm and legs. A frenzied killing. One hit could have killed her, but she had endured nine. Nine stabbings. Nine deep holes puncturing her tiny brown body.

Lowe rushed to her, screaming, crying, shocked. At just sixteen, she had looked into the dead eyes of her sister. As she knelt, hugging Shannon's tiny frame that laid helplessly killed, instant survivor's guilt spread over Lowe.

Police had eventually come to rescue her, after a neighbour called them upon hearing her screams. They pulled her from that dingy flat,

33

covered in her family's blood. From then on, she was left to the system.

Hayes had seen the file. These dealers had beaten, stabbed and killed both her sister and her mother and then disappeared. They were never caught, and they got away with what they did. To this day, Lowe carried the regret of not being home that day. She'd have at least been able to save Shannon if she'd have been there, she was sure of it.

By eighteen, Lowe had lost everything and everyone. She was on her own. Everyone who was supposed to care for her was either dead or had abandoned her, and she'd sworn to herself that from then on, she would never let anyone hurt her again.

Luckily, she had the determination to get herself out of there. With support from her school, she won a scholarship and was able to further her education. She had always been clever and now her circumstances and exposure to the harshness of the world had set her on a path to ensure justice. Ultimately, that was how she ended up the Detective Chief Inspector she was today – eighteen years later.

Hayes couldn't even begin to imagine how she'd overcome it. He was one of the very few people to know her history and felt privileged that she had shared it with him. They'd been colleagues for a long time. She'd been by his side as he married his wife, Molly and as they welcomed both his sons into the world. In a way, she was a part of his family, but understandably, she'd always kept a comfortable distance. It also meant he knew never to comment on issues that may provoke painful memories of the past.

They walked for moment in silence.

'They're saying the husband will probably come around after surgery...' he started up.

'Any news on the girl?' Lowe asked, entirely dismissive of information on Joseph.

'We got a name,' Hayes looked to his partner.

'Oh?'

'Anna Miller.'

The Aftermath

With nothing left to do but wait, Elizabeth returned home...or to the crime scene. It didn't feel like a home to her. Just a collection of big empty rectangles with characterless furniture. Elizabeth set down her bag and for no reason at all, walked about the house looking over rooms numbly. Eventually, she went down to see the mess that had been left now that the crime investigation team had finished.

The once busy setting of important activity now remained stagnant and still. There were bits of tape, plastic and dust on the floor where the forensics team had been working. Nothing but the mattress was left on the bed, and it, along with the floorboards, remained soaked with the horrifyingly crimson stains of three people, marking the bloody battle.

Elizabeth stared into the room coldly. How could she be expected to stay here? Alone. Sleeping in the aftermath of Eddy's gruesome death. The family liaison officer had given her the number of a team that would clean it up for her. She'd give them a call right away. She couldn't have her kids coming home to see it. It would also give her something to do whilst she waited. She left the basement and returned to the upper living areas of the house, closing the door behind her. With that, she wanted to be done. She would not go in that room again.

How, in so little time, had her life changed so drastically?

Elizabeth picked up her handbag and went up to her bedroom. She kicked off her shoes and made the first of three phone calls. The first was to the cleaning company, with whom she arranged a time the next day for them to visit. She wanted it sorted as quickly as possible. The second to her son who, although shocked, was level-headed and asked if his mother wanted him to come home. Of course, she told him this wouldn't be necessary, although really all she wanted was someone to be with her. The final and hardest call was to her daughter. The questions were harder to satisfy than she anticipated. The "what happened?", the "is he OK?", the "what did she do?". The answer to all being a raw "I don't know."

As the heart wrenching calls ended, Elizabeth threw down her phone onto the bed. She didn't wish to speak to anyone else. She lay down on her pillow and stared blankly into space for a long while until the darkness drew in. She didn't sleep. How could she?

She sat up slowly and reached for her bag.

***

Lowe found herself accidentally at Rob's door again, for the second evening. She knocked. He answered. She went in. The same as always. It seemed whenever she felt stressed, frustrated, confused, upset, or sometimes even excited with a case, he was her outlet. At first it was great, exciting, fun. Two years later, he felt like a fool.

He went over to the kitchen to put the kettle on as she made herself comfy in the lounge. He looked across the counter to see her switching on the news.

'Your place not come with TV?' he asked, handing her a cup of tea.

She didn't reply. She was watching the report on her case. Sometimes the news helped. Sometimes they just made it worse. She knew it was going to be a public case, so she had to be ready. Rob looked over and caught the gist of what was going on.

'This your case?'

'Yeah.'

'Is it… you want to talk about it?' he asked. He wasn't ever really sure what to say when she was focused on a case. She sipped her tea, still watching. Her mind consumed by the story. He may as well have not been there. He sighed.

'You could let me know when you're coming over you know?'

She said nothing. He took the remote and switched off the TV. She turned to him aggressively. He didn't care, it was his place. He stared at her, waiting for her to give in.

'Fine. How was your day?' she played along, replying sarcastically.

'How was yours?'

'Normal, just a new case. That one…I was trying to–'

'You're not at work anymore. Let it go.' He looked to her disapprovingly, leaning back.

'Let it go? A man is dead Rob.'

'I'm in corporate finance. I practically work with dead people every day,' he said humorously. She wanted to throw a clever retort back at him, but instead she released a laugh. He smiled at her, enjoying the sound of her laughter, before supportively adding, 'You'll crack it, you always do. Whatever it takes.'

She smiled thoughtfully back at him, but it faded the moment the image of the bloodied blonde lying lifelessly on the bed flashed into her mind.

The Media

'Have you seen this?!' Hayes swivelled on his chair across to where Lowe was examining photos and documents of things taken from the scene. He thrust a newspaper down in front of her. She turned towards him, picking it up and reading the headline: "Star Doctor Attacked by Crazy Fan".

'Fucking tabloids,' she spat. No definitive narrative had been agreed upon yet and certainly no one from their end had suggested this to any member of the press. Not to mention it was grossly inaccurate. Lowe skimmed through the offensive number of lies in the article.

'I'm guessing a few of the neighbours wanted their five minutes of fame.' She handed the far-fetched newspaper back to her partner, unamused.

'So not the wife?'

'I get the feeling she isn't a fan of having her privacy invaded...'

'Makes you wonder what we pay the bloody Press Officers for right?' Hayes scoffed. Lowe was about to respond, when the deep imposing voice of Detective Superintendent Mark Tabbot commanded their presence.

'You two, my office, now!'

Obeying orders like two teenagers summoned by the head teacher, Lowe and Hayes dragged their feet into the corner office belonging to their clearly pissed off superintendent. He slumped down into his black leather desk chair and turned to face them. Before he could start, Lowe placed the copy of the newspaper onto the desk in front of him, correctly anticipating what he was about to say.

'We've seen it.' She crossed her arms.

'High-profile,' Tabbot cocked a brow. 'Not good for us. Chief wants status updates daily.'

'Sir, we believe some neighbours may have suspicioned and sold the story,' Hayes offered.

'There isn't any evidence yet to say she was the attacker, Sir,' Lowe chimed in, expanding further, 'we've found no signs of forced entry, so she must have been invited in. She's also sustained greater injuries. It looks like it might be messier than–'

'This is a favourable narrative…' Tabbot interjected, pointing to the paper.

'Sir, it's unlikely that's what happened,' Lowe advised, irritated.

'We need to respond with comment to the press. We can't bide our time with crimes like this, in neighbourhoods like that, involving people like him,' Tabbot warned, but noticing the repugnant expression spreading across Lowe's face, he cautiously added, 'Chief's words, not mine. What d'you have?'

At that moment Hayes' phone rung, interrupting the friction in the room.

'Ooh, sorry, excuse me.' He took it out of his pocket and hurried out of the office to take the call, leaving Lowe and Tabbot to discuss. He was honestly quite relieved to be out of the room. He'd noticed that this particular case had put Lowe on edge so far. Her temperament was shorter and what some may call more volatile, but he preferred to see it as determined. Either way, he didn't want to be the fly on the wall when Tabbot forced her to investigate it as a "crazy fan attacking a celebrity".

Back inside the office however, Lowe was unwavering.

'Sir, if I may. We have reason to believe it may have been attempted sexual assault that went wrong,' she stood firmly. Tabbot's eyes widened with surprise.

'On what grounds?'

'Well...' Lowe was slightly more hesitant being questioned by her superior but also acutely aware that her argument was primarily based on her own intuition. 'There were two middle-aged men and a young female found in a bedroom. She sustained more injuries than this "celebrity" doctor, who was found on top of her on a bed in a basement. From experience Sir, the circumstances suggest–'

'Any physical evidence?' Again, Tabbot cocked an eyebrow, waiting for a response. Lowe looked upwards, her arms uncrossing and flinging to her side.

'No,' she answered resentfully through gritted teeth. She was waiting on the evidence. 'But–'

'Get back to work DCI Lowe.'

'But Sir, I–' Lowe protested, but, as was becoming a habit, her sentence was cut off almost immediately.

'NO!' Tabbot shot up, raising his voice. With both hands firmly on his desk, he looked her square in the eye. 'You've got nothing. You're walking on thin ice here Detective...'

Regretting his overreaction immediately, he sank back into his chair and rubbed his forehead. Lowe was taken aback. His reaction, much like her own, seemed most over the top and out of character.

'Look, the Chief isn't about to let the press loose with another unverified sexual assault accusation against a man of high status. We can't deal with the publicity right now. Y'know it's like a witch hunt these days...' he explained himself, massaging his brow.

A small part of Lowe understood the pressure and scrutiny her boss was under – that they were all under – with a high-profile case involving a "celebrity". Lowe chose to use the term sparingly, since it seemed anyone with their photograph online could be called that these days. The problem was, that kind of pressure didn't matter to her. That part of the job was far too small to outweigh the gross sense of injustice that emanated from ignoring the fact a person was wrongfully harmed, just to avoid some negative press.

She would never understand why people in positions of power, those who have sworn to protect citizens, were far more concerned with office politics and public image than actually doing the right thing. That backwards mindset had cost her dearly in the past. The irony was perhaps that in doing the right thing, these people may have had a better public image and reputation amongst colleagues. She was bewildered by the fact that they hadn't yet figured this out, let alone not realising that they were ethically wrong.

Furthermore, why was Tabbot so quick to dismiss sexual assault being part of this investigation? Why couldn't a woman like Anna Miller be given the benefit of the doubt, especially when it seemed like Lowe was being asked by her superiors to give this Doctor J. Warren it?

Of course, there are always going to be people who cry wolf but anyone who makes false allegations, in Lowe's opinion, deserved to be punished, just as the culprits themselves should be. Those who spread false indictments are not only wasting police time and damaging the wrongly accused, but they are hindering and altering the future attitudes of officers when dealing with real and serious allegations.

Throughout history, genuine victims of sexual assault, especially women, have struggled and fought to be believed, but the moment just one single person tells a lie and puts in one false claim, progress darts backwards by decades.

Even now, Tabbot was asking Lowe to extend consideration for the man involved over and above the woman. Except, that logic didn't apply for this instance. Anna Miller hadn't made a claim. Neither had Joseph Warren. Lowe, as an experienced detective, was just interpreting what she'd seen at the scene.

Nevertheless, the system remained that without solid evidence, it was likely already a waste of resource for Lowe to continue down that avenue. It didn't matter if there were circumstances to suggest Anna had been harmed. That wasn't the bottom line for her superiors. Closing the case quickly and not attracting further media attention was. Well, Lowe wasn't about to let that pressure influence her. She was going to find the evidence she needed to prove she was right and make sure the young woman involved received the justice she deserved.

Lowe was on the brink of unleashing the thoughts burning inside her mind, when Hayes knocked and re-entered the room, distracting her completely.

'Warren's awake. We should go,' he informed her, seeking dismissal from Tabbot, who nodded in agreement. Lowe turned to leave with her partner, but before she could Tabbot slammed his finger down on the newspaper article.

'And Abigail, use this to appeal for witnesses. Anyone who may have seen something. Get us a narrative. End of the day.'

She nodded, agreeing. That would have to wait. Right now, something far more important was occupying her mind. The pure and provoked determination to find evidential proof.

The Suspect

In a large private room, Joseph had come around and was recovering well from his minor surgery. When the detectives entered, he was propped up on the bed, with the small table pulled across the centre. Atop it, some unappealing hospital food sat half eaten on a seafoam green tray, alongside a few newspapers and a cheap mobile phone. He, himself was reading one of the newspapers where he'd made front-page news, which he placed down nonchalantly upon seeing the two detectives.

'Ah, hello!' he greeted them warmly, 'I've been waiting for you, please have a seat.'

Hayes sat in the large-backed, pink leather chair beside Joseph's hospital bed and rested his elbows on the wooden arms. Lowe opted to remain standing at the foot of the bed.

'Thank you for coming so soon.' Joseph smiled at them.

'How are you feeling?' Hayes began, indifferent to the man.

'Well, I'll admit I've been better,' Joseph chuckled lightly gesturing to his current position. 'I'll be OK, really. Should be out of here in a few days or so I reckon and then with just a few weeks recovery, I'll be back on the job in no time, just this time I'll be the one saving lives!' Joseph beamed proudly.

How modest, thought Lowe sarcastically.

'We're glad to hear it. Now, obviously, you know why we're here, we'd like to ask what happened, if you're ready to talk to us?' Hayes continued, much more open and quickly swayed by the doctor's oh-so charming personality.

'Of course, yes! I understand. I'll do whatever I can to help and get charges pressed against that horrible woman.' Joseph bore his gritted teeth when referring to the "horrible woman".

'What charges?' Lowe's dark eyebrows raised so high they nearly disappeared into her hair. Until then, she'd been watching him intently, registering his body language. He seemed laid back. Casual. Unaffected. It was not the way someone who had been the victim of a crime would typically behave. They'd be tense, anxious, scared and often a weird mixture of upset or angry.

'Assault I'm guessing? I'm not sure what it would be called, isn't that your job?' He turned to her, brushing off the question in a somewhat patronising manner, which only served to convince Lowe further of his guilt.

'Uh... in your own time Doctor Warren, if you could take us through the events as they occurred on the evening of the twenty-fourth?' Hayes asked politely.

Joseph willingly switched his attention to the more receptive male detective beside him.

'No problem, and I apologise for getting uppity. The medication makes me a little...' he turned momentarily towards Lowe with a subtle smirk that was meant only for her, '...irritable.'

Lowe narrowed her eyes and threw back a forced and clearly fake smile. She didn't like him. She probably should have given him the benefit of the doubt, but currently she felt unwilling to do so and his behaviour wasn't helping.

'Understandable,' Hayes, blissfully oblivious to the tone of their exchanges, offered him sympathy.

In his mind, it was understandable for Joseph to be snappy. Many victims of crimes had odd reactions because of medications – in particular those on pain relief. Perhaps he had been trying to save face before and underneath was hurting and stressed. At the very least, he thought, his partner could give this man a chance to offer his side of the story. They had no way of knowing yet what happened in that room, so it was wrong to make assumptions too early, as he'd pointed out to his partner. Joseph hadn't come across like a typical perp anyway. There was always the chance Lowe was wrong.

Being close to her, Hayes knew that a lifetime's worth of interactions with men had taught her to be naturally cautious and distrustful, but when it came to her job she needed to let go of her bias. They weren't all bad. He liked to think of himself as a good, respectable family man, and his wife would surely agree. There was every possibility that Lowe had drawn her conclusions too early. Perhaps this seemingly nice man they were questioning was innocent in all this.

On the other hand, maybe Lowe was right, and Joseph would try and falsify his testimony in a bid to victimise himself and get off scot-free. He could have been at fault. He could have been the one that hurt the other two people in that room.

Either way, they would need to err on the side of caution and Hayes knew that Lowe would be listening like a bat to every individual word that came out of his mouth, ready to call him out on any inconsistencies. Though he couldn't pinpoint what it was exactly, he knew something was viscerally bothering her about this case, and it was making her overly reactive. He needed to support her by ensuring Joseph and other witnesses remained cooperative and was sorry if Lowe felt that he was undermining her at times.

'So, can you take us through what happened on the evening of the twenty-fourth?' Hayes repeated, adding a warm smile, which was reciprocated. Luckily, Hayes didn't have to try too hard. The man wanted to talk.

'The papers aren't far off. Eddy and I – that is Edward Braithwaite – were meeting that evening for drinks, just one or two at Zero, before and he was going to come back to look over my latest paper. Eddy is a professor at the Imperial, I often ask for his opinion,' Joseph launched into his story.

'Just to clarify at this point, what is your relation to Edward Braithwaite?' Hayes asked.

'We went to University together. We remained friends all these years. He lives close by.' He rushed through his answer, desperate to get back to his rehearsed narrative.

'Anyway, we went for drinks, Eddy picked me up and we went down there at about eight or eight thirty. I don't remember exactly. We had a few drinks, which turned into a few more, you know how it goes. We ended up chatting to a couple of girls in the bar–'

'Did you know any of the women?' Lowe cut in.

'No, no. They were strangers. Pleasant enough. Eddy never married, so I let him have a bit of fun. I wingman him every so often, it helps, with me being on TV and such.'

Lowe rolled her eyes. 'Do you remember any of their names?'

'Ooh, uhm only first names maybe.' He stopped to think for a moment. He hadn't been prepared to answer this question. 'There was a Liz or Liv or something like that, a Courtney, Anna or Hannah and a couple of others I didn't get the name of. There were a group of about four or five of them. They were having drinks after work. It was all good.

'I'd wanted to head off earlier, to get to the paper but we'd stayed late by then, it was about ten or half ten. We'd decided to leave the research paper to another night... because it was late, and I wanted to be up in the morning to see my wife. She'd been away with my children, at our place in France. As we were leaving, one of the girls, this Hannah–'

'Anna,' Lowe corrected him.

'Anna. She wanted to leave early too. We'd had a nice time and she'd been getting on with Eddy. She was a little drunk, a bit underdressed for winter in just a dress, so we asked what direction she was heading. Since she was going our way, we offered her a lift, no point in her paying for a cab all by herself, you know how much that costs here! We thought we would do the nice thing.

'So, like I said, we offered her the lift to the station, she was unsure at first, not wanting to trouble us, but we insisted, chivalry and all that. Something I will live to regret, let me tell you. Anyway, my house was closest, so Eddy dropped me home first. Thought that may also give him a chance to go on with her, get lucky, if you know what I mean. When we got there, this Anna said she needed to use the toilet and was desperate. Seeing no trouble with it, I let her in to use the toilet. Once inside, I took her through to show her where the bathroom was on that level of the house, just down from my study, but she suddenly threw herself at me. I mean, I was shocked.'

'Threw herself in what way?' Hayes asked for clarification.

'Uhm. Sexually. She tried to kiss me and put her body against mine, pushing me into the study – it's also a bedroom but I am a married man and she was quite drunk, so I tried to get her off. When I rejected her, she started to get violent. She was hitting me. Knocking things. Screaming. Broke a glass tumbler I hadn't taken back to the kitchen yet. I was uncomfortable to be honest. I regretted letting her in.'

'Then what happened? How did you get to the state we found you in?'

'Well she grabbed a pair of scissors! She was very angry about being rejected. It was at that point that Eddy came in. I guess he wondered what was taking so long. I rushed to try and get something to protect myself as he tried to stop her. I grabbed a hammer, it was the first thing I could get hold of. Eddy had tried to overpower her, but she attacked him, and he fell over in the corner.

'I tried to get the scissors off her, tried to defend myself against them with the hammer. Knocked her onto the bed in the process, there was a bit of a struggle. I felt a sharp pain in my stomach, and then everything blacked out. Next thing, I wake up here, all stitched up.' He finished his account of the story. It took a moment for all the information to settle in.

'That was detailed, thank you for going over this for us,' Hayes gave a reassuring look to Joseph, who was now resting against the back of the bed, a little sweaty from his animated account.

'That's the truth. I'm sure you've spoken to Eddy, he'll confirm it I'm sure,' Joseph offered, when neither of the two detectives said much more for a moment.

Lowe and Hayes exchanged an awkward glance at the statement, suddenly realising that Joseph was missing a crucial piece of information about the event. Instantly Lowe knew that this missing piece of information would depict him as innocent. This would prove a problem for her theory.

'Doctor Warren, have you spoken to your wife yet?' Hayes asked, realising that they would have to be the ones to apparently deliver the bad news.

'No, I haven't had the chance, I don't know where she is, I assume she's gone home to sleep or talk to the kids, perhaps get the place cleaned up, she is always cleaning, my wife. Why? What's wrong?' he asked, flicking between the two in search of an answer.

Lowe bit her lip and looked to Hayes. He took the hint and leant forward.

'Uhm, Joseph, your friend Eddy, he uhm, he didn't make it I'm afraid. We're ever so sorry.'

'What? No. He. What? How?' His sudden panic-stricken reaction was convincing.

'He uh, he lost too much blood and one of the wounds was so deep, his rib punctured his lung the paramedics said. He was already dead, before ambulances arrived at the scene. We're truly sorry. We offer our sincerest condolences.' Hayes took a deep breath.

Joseph sunk into the bed, shock seemingly setting in. It was time they left him alone to process this news.

'We're going to leave you to it, we'll get the officer outside to call your wife, so you can be with her. We can get a grief counsellor if you would like?' Hayes stood up ready to leave.

'No. No. Just call my wife,' Joseph exhaled emotionally.

'We will and thank you for the information you've provided today.' Hayes put his hand to Joseph's arm momentarily. A small signifier of thanks and sorrow for the man.

'Just one last thing, if that's OK?' Lowe remembered before leaving the room. She herself wasn't sure whether he'd already known if his friend was dead or not. His response seemed so authentic. Organic. Even to her. He couldn't be that convincing of an actor, could he?

Joseph looked up, grief-stricken but willing to respond. Lowe tried to form her question.

'On your computer, there was some kind of video or camera that had been ejected, there was a cable and a program open...'

'Oh, yeah, I'd just been using it to upload medical pictures and scans from my phone for the paper earlier in the afternoon. The program always opens when I do that, like some auto-media thing. I always forget to close it.' Joseph's simple, yet believable answer completely destroyed Lowe's line of thought when it came to the camera. She would have to let that one go. His statement was their only lead for now.

'Thank you,' She nodded sceptically, before both the detectives finally left the room. Joseph remained stationary, left to process the news of losing his oldest friend.

***

Once outside, Hayes took a deep breath and asked the officer outside to get someone to call Joseph's wife. They were done with him for now. He turned to his partner.

'I read Miller's medical reports this morning, her blood alcohol was significantly high, it checks out with the scene, same weapons, same positions, we can check with the bar to confirm they were there. Everything lines up I'd say.'

'Just one thing... if they'd had lots of drinks, why on earth was the vic driving? Why would an educated man and doctor let a drunk person drive himself and another home? Bit irresponsible, no?'

'I mean, c'mon Abs, the guy is dead. Murdered by the sounds of it. Do you really want to issue him with a posthumous drink-driving charge? It's not the point here. You know that. I know you don't want to admit it, but everything else makes sense; it's clear, detailed, consistent with the findings at the scene. He doesn't seem to have any motivation to lie. If he had done something, I'm pretty sure he would have known his friend was dead. He wouldn't have reacted like that. What d'you think?' Hayes reasoned with her.

'After hearing his story?' Lowe exhaled, unsure now of what to believe. She turned to her partner, reluctant to give up on her instincts just yet. 'Either he's telling the truth or he's a fucking good liar.'

'What do you want to do?'

It was a weighted question from Hayes. Lowe would now have to decide whether that was the narrative she wanted to lock in and follow, ready to give to her superiors. Everything he'd said had made sense. He'd not left room for many questions. As Hayes noted, it was clear, detailed and could likely be corroborated. It wouldn't be the first time a drunk fangirl tried to throw herself at a TV star and it certainly wouldn't be the last. His motivations for inviting her in made sense.

Lowe exhaled, put her hand on her hips and answered Hayes, 'Let's cuff the girl until she wakes up. Let Tabbot know, he'll be happy.'

Even as she made the decision and the instructions fell out of her mouth, there was a small gut wrenching feeling that she could not shake. The feeling that reminded her of the young woman who was yet to awaken. The thought of her lying unresponsive and bleeding on that bed, just like her sister had all those years ago on the kitchen floor. Her sister, whose killer was never caught or sentenced.

Lowe's phone vibrated, diverting her thoughts. She yanked it out of her pocket, saw Rob was calling and silenced it. Hayes looked at the phone curiously but did not ask. They then walked through the corridors of Charing Cross Hospital to the room where Anna Miller remained in a coma, her future uncertain.

When they entered, Hayes looked over the excess of medical equipment attached to the woman. Breathing tubes were connected to a large grey box that seemed to huff out air every time it raised and sunk, similar to how his wife huffed every time he went home and turned on the sports channel. Multiple cannulas connected to multiple transparent tubes, which in turn met heavy bags of fluid. A carefully ordered assortment of wires assembled over her chest, monitoring her heart. And underneath it all, Anna.

Lowe reluctantly fixed the patient's wrist to the bed with handcuffs.

She looked to Hayes as he mused over the ECG print beside her, not really knowing what he was looking at. 'Any response yet?'

'No... d'you think she'll pull through?'

'I hope so Hayes; she's our prime suspect now.'

The Decision

It had been an exhausting few days with the case and Lowe was feeling a mixture of emotions, which she desperately needed a release from. Like always, there was only one place she knew to go for that.

She knocked on his door.

Moments later, Rob appeared, pulling the door ajar. He looked down to see her standing there, that fierce look in her eyes. He hadn't expected her, but then it wasn't unusual for her to show up without warning. She always did.

Lowe looked up to him expectantly. He knew what would happen. The same thing that always happened. She would throw herself at him, he would resist a little but give in. He couldn't help it, he wanted her. He loved the feeling of her being close to him. As soon as she touched him, his resistance dissolved like a bath bomb hitting the water.

It wasn't just the sex; he liked everything about her. He loved that she was a strong, confident woman who knew how to take care of herself. He loved that she was intelligent, that she worked hard, and she had this dark sense of humour that occasionally came out and matched his own. Most of all, he loved those rare moments where she would let down her guard and be herself, although those were few and far between.

She was a heavily shielded person. Private. Unpredictable. He couldn't read her, and she never offered anything. He'd deduced that there was something in her past that had made her this way, maybe a guy had hurt her somewhere down the road. He knew she had trouble trusting people. He knew any form of a connection made her feel defenceless and insecure. She didn't want to be vulnerable, she refused to be, but he tried to be persistent with her. He had to be.

They'd reached a point where she'd at least stay until the morning, but after that she'd be gone. She'd ignore his calls and messages and give him nothing. He would be alone, yearning for more. For that deeper connection he so desperately wanted, from a woman who seemed incapable of giving it. Therein lied the problem.

He was getting older now and wanted to settle down, he couldn't keep being her scapegoat. He wanted more, and if she couldn't give it, he needed to move on. It was time. He couldn't let her keep walking over him and hurting him. He couldn't let her break his heart over and over again. It was time for her to make a decision: commit or bail.

Her showing up like this just made it harder.

She walked straight in, taking off her jacket, and pushing her lips towards his. He met her enthusiastically, allowing himself to be led across the apartment to the bed. He was giving in – again. After she'd left and ignored him – again. He let her hands pull up his t-shirt and assisted her, pulling it over his head. She unbuttoned her shirt, her weight pressing against his as they fell onto the bed. He gave in. He wanted her and, in this moment at least, she wanted him.

They had sex.

Afterwards, she lay on her stomach, looking away from him in thought. He traced her spine with his finger, watching her, willing her to turn, to make some connection with him.

'You can stop that,' she said softly. Obligated, he took his hand away and huffed back onto his side of the bed – the left.

'I want more,' he blurted out.

Lowe closed her eyes momentarily and sat up, her back still to him. 'Not this again Rob, we've been through this,' she stroked her hairline.

'No. You've dodged it. Every time,' he corrected her brusquely. She reached for her shirt and pulled it around herself.

'Oh what, so now you're leaving?' He watched her as she slipped on her trousers and stood up, finally facing him.

'Look, Robert, I–'

'Robert?' He raised his eyebrows in disbelief. She tilted her head to the side. She really just needed the release. She didn't need him to feel anything more. It was purely physical. That was all. She went to reply but he stopped her.

He stood up to face her, the sheets covering him. 'I've been patient Abbie, I have, and I don't mean to make you uncomfortable or put you on the spot, but it's time. I want to be with you. And I want you to want to be with me, but if you're not ready, it's time I move on. I want a family, I want to settle down. You've got to decide; you want to give this a go or not? I mean, I get if you're not there. It'll hurt, but I get it. And that's fine. But I need to know…'

Lowe was lost for words. She knew he was within his right to ask, but she didn't know what to say to him. She wasn't there yet. At least she was pretty sure she wasn't.

Maybe it was time to let him move on.

He walked around the bed to her, still holding the sheets around his waist and looked her directly in her "deer-in-headlights" eyes.

'Take your time. That's all I've got to say; my cards are on the table,' Rob finished, gave her a quick kiss on the forehead and went for a shower.

Lowe remained hovering on the spot, his ultimatum hanging over her.

The Post-Mortem

The next day, Lowe and Hayes pulled up ready for the post-mortem on Ed Braithwaite. The medical examiner pulled back the noisy plastic sheet from the greying corpse lying on the cold metallic table. Lowe retched in her mouth, whilst Hayes screwed up his face as the smell washed over them. Dead people really didn't smell good and this was undoubtedly one of the worst parts of the job, but also one of the most necessary.

'What's the damage?' Hayes asked the clichéd lab-coated, glasses-wearing examiner, who moved about the body unphased to begin pointing at wounds.

'Right, we've got fractures on the skull, trauma from possibly a blunt mid-weight object to the parietal and frontal temporal regions. Bruising in multiple places, as you can see. Main trauma occurred on the sternum, with damage, breakages and splintering on the left, fifth through to eighth ribs and damage to costal cartilage. Wounds caused extensive bleeding by time the body was found. Pneumothorax present in left side also. Either could have been the cause of fatality…' She spoke quickly without taking a breath, until she looked up to see both detectives staring at her, dumbfounded.

They'd had trouble keeping up with her pace, let alone understanding her complex vocabulary. They both watched her, hoping for a further elaboration of her findings, but in layman's terms.

'Sorry...' she chuckled sheepishly, looking at the floor and pulling at her sleeve. 'This is only like my third homicide assessment.'

'Everybody has to start somewhere,' Lowe offered a reassuring smile.

'D'you mind translating for us simpletons please?' Hayes asked warmly. She beamed back, glad to be so well received by these two experienced detectives. She was undoubtedly nervous, which probably attributed to how fast she had spoken. She took a breath and started over.

'Um, the victim's skull is fractured on the top of the head, with denting and severe bruising on the front and left-hand side, here...' She touched the corpse with her gloved finger to show them where, and they followed her, taking it in. 'I suspect this trauma is from possibly a blunt mid-weight object. Same object used below on the torso.' She moved down to the chest and stomach area, where deep dry wounds were clearly visible. Even though the staff in the coroner's office had done their best to patch up the body, it still looked like someone had mutilated the entire left side of the man.

'Cause of death?' Lowe inquired.

'Hard to call exactly, he would have been bleeding out pretty bad, there must have been three or four hits to the stomach. They're massive wounds. Did a lot of internal damage. Someone would have pulled the object out repeatedly too, as most of the breakage points are from the inside of the rib, with splintering protruding outwards. Um, that's why I think pronged or curved object, personally. However, he also had a punctured lung, it's hard to call exactly which would have drained first. Either could have been the cause of fatality… I think the pneumo…uh, punctured lung resulting from sustained injuries would be cause of death. We've got a few scans left to run this afternoon to determine this for sure, which will be added to the report we'll send over.'

'The object… would scissors fit?' Hayes said, thinking of the pair that had been stuck into the other two people involved and also in the testimony given by Warren.

'Like house scissors?' she asked. Hayes gave a nod. The examiner searched her brain and began shaking her head.

'I don't think so. Too thin and sharp. They wouldn't produce wounds like this.'

'How about a hammer?' Lowe tried, knowing this would tie Joseph to these injuries. By his own account he had placed the hammer in his own hands.

'Yep. That would be the most probable object. It's the one I most suspect. A horrible way to die. It would have taken some strength. This couldn't happen accidentally…' the examiner began.

'Great, thank you,' Lowe cut in, stopping her from babbling on but also giving her an appreciative nod.

Lowe looked over the torso once more, holding her breath to counteract the smell. 'Oh, if the dead could talk…' she muttered almost inaudibly under her breath, as she began piecing the puzzle of the twenty-fourth together in her mind.

Anna Miller couldn't have weighed more than seventy kilograms fully clothed, and she'd looked so weak lying there on the bed in that room. In Lowe's mind, there was no way she could have caused those injuries. Even if she had grabbed the hammer at some point, she couldn't have been strong enough, could she? Sure, there was always the added strength from adrenaline and it wasn't impossible, but realistically it just didn't seem likely.

The woman was not the guilty party. Lowe was convinced of it. No matter what Joseph Warren had said. Unfortunately, without Anna's testimony, she would have to wait for the forensics evidence to come back to confirm who held the hammer that killed Ed Braithwaite.

'We'll need that report as soon as you're done here. Thanks for having us in.' Hayes was just finishing the meeting by shaking the examiner's hand when Lowe walked out purposefully.

She'd made a mistake in letting Hayes convince her that Joseph was telling the truth, resulting in her handcuffing Anna Miller and right now, she needed to find hard evidence to reverse it.

The Bar

For a start, gaining CCTV footage from the bar would help give the detectives some indication of how the events began to unfold on the evening of the twenty-fourth. It would be the most useful evidence in their investigation so far, until the forensics taken from the scene were finished undergoing analysis. That, and the results of the kit she'd requested to be performed on Anna Miller. Lowe secretly hoped that the results would support her theory about what happened.

When they arrived at the bar, it was closed, so they went around to the side alley to find workers taking in a delivery.

'Uh, excuse me?' Lowe called to them over the noise of heavy barrels being unloaded. A man, of around thirty years old, wearing old blue jeans and a simple black t-shirt, looked up from a barrel.

'Hi, I'm Detective Lowe and this is my partner Detective Hayes...'.

'Right, yeah, what can I do for you?' the man wiped sweat from his brow. He seemed indifferent to them. In the capital it wasn't unusual for the police to approach a bar in the course of an investigation.

'We're looking for the manager…d'you know where we would be able to find–'

'That's me, Jack Walker, hi.'

The man, now identified as Jack Walker, manager of Zero, walked forward, wiped his hand on his jeans and outstretched it to the detectives. Noticing the sweaty palms, Lowe hesitated but was relieved when Hayes met the man's hand with his own to shake it.

'What can I do you for?'

'We're after some CCTV…if that's OK?' Lowe asked, hoping that he would be receptive. He eyed the them up. A part of him wanted to ask what it was regarding, but from experience he knew that if he wanted to sleep at night, he'd rather not know.

'For sure. Come on in.' Jack led them through the side entrance and into the bar.

It was a surprisingly neat, upmarket bar, the kind that sported those low hanging industrials bulbs which floated over the bar with glowing gentrification. The furniture was mismatched, with metallic shades of black, blue and bronze, the wooden top of the bar contrasted with the black iron foot and sides.

'Can I get you a drink?' Jack interrupted Lowe taking in her surroundings.

'Uh…no, thank you.'

'And you Sir?' he looked to Hayes, pouring neat brown fluid into two glasses without waiting for the answer. 'So what date are we looking at. We've got front entrance and bar camera, plus outside near the toilets, side entrance…we're pretty secure in here. Don't need no trouble.'

He was surprisingly upbeat for an early morning. Then again, the drinking before midday may have had something to do with that. Either way, thought Lowe as she joined Hayes at the bar, he was being helpful, and that was useful for them.

'Twenty-fourth, around eight to eleven maybe. We're looking for these people specifically,' Lowe explained, taking out three photos from her inside jacket pocket. She placed the photos of Joseph Warren, Ed Braithwaite and Anna Miller on the bar in front of Jack. He put his drink down under her nose. As she caught a whiff of the strong liquor, she heaved uncontrollably, causing alarm in both men.

'You alright there, Love?' Jack looked at her slightly worried, more so about the fact that it was far too early for him to be cleaning up someone's sick. Lowe stood up from the stool, holding her stomach.

'Yeah… uh… one too many hangovers on that stuff,' she smiled unconvincingly. 'I'm going to get some air. You OK to get this?' she asked Hayes, trying to compose herself.

'Course…' he nodded, concerned.

Lowe went back outside to the side alley, where workers were still unloading barrels. She breathed in. Maybe she was overtired, she hadn't slept well the night before. Maybe she was still feeling sick from the overwhelming scent of the corpse. Either way, she was glad to be outside. Waiting for her partner, she checked her phone, somewhat hopefully, for messages. She had none.

Inside, Hayes turned back to the bar manager.

'Women 'ey? Lightweights.' Jack commented, before switching his attention back to the photos. He picked up the headshot of Joseph. 'Yeah, I recognise this guy. He's on the TV, right? He was here, with another bloke. I guess that one…' he indicated to the photo of Ed. 'Uh, they were with a bunch of girls, on the curve of the bar that end.'

'Was she one of them?' Hayes asked, holding up the photo of Anna. Jack scanned through his memory.

'She could have been, I don't know man. I see so many faces. Hard to tell. The friend was more interested in the girls, this guy seemed more reserved, like he didn't say much, just kinda watched them. Pretty intense really. The girls were nice, drunk quite a bit. Good for business. A couple of them left earlier I think, maybe three, stayed on. That's about as specific as I can be, maybe one of the staff noticed more, but I doubt it, it was a busy night.'

'That's OK, thanks. Can I get a look at the CCTV?'

'Oh right, the tapes, sure. Evening of the twenty-fourth you say?'

'Yeah, that's right.' Hayes got up ready to follow Jack to view the tapes.

'Uh, do you mind if I make you a copy? I'm pretty busy, delivery was late. I don't mean to be a pain. Will take a few minutes to burn, you can watch me do it, so you know I'm not like manipulating them or nought.'

'Oh, no, not at all, now would be great, thanks! We'd ask for one anyway, so yeah, a copy now would be good,' Hayes said, grateful that the manager was being so open and helpful. He followed him through to a small security room out back, where Jack burned a copy of the CCTV footage for them and handed it over without hesitation.

'Sorry I'm so busy man, I just really gotta get this done, but look anything you need, just give me a call. Happy to help.' Jack reached inside his pocket and pulled out a slightly damaged business card. Hayes took it.

'Thanks, you've been a real help. Uh, we'll probably need you to go and give a witness statement at the station on record at some point, just head down, tell them it's for the Doctor J. Warren case.'

'For sure. I'm off tomorrow so I'll head down and do that.'

'Great, and thank you, for this.' Hayes held up the tape.

'I hope it helps with whatever you're looking for.' Jack smiled, showing the detective out, glad to be rid of them so he could continue the delivery. Truly, he was incredibly busy and short-staffed that morning.

Outside, CCTV footage in hand, Hayes re-joined his colleague, who was standing watching life go by on the street outside.

'Hey, you OK?' His concern was genuine.

'Yeah, yeah. I'm fine. Just a flashback to my younger days. Anytime I smell whiskey now, my gag reflex has a party,' she explained. Hayes narrowed his eyes, still unconvinced. He'd never noticed that before. Observing his scepticism, Lowe assured him once more, 'I'm OK, I promise. Did you get the footage?'

'I did.'

'Well then, let's go see how it all started.'

The CCTV

Back at the station, Lowe and Hayes ingested the CCTV footage. It would, at the very least, give them an indication of how the three came together in the first place, whilst they waited on forensics to come back and Anna Miller to – they hoped – come out of her coma.

'You ready?' Hayes asked, sitting down next to Lowe, ready to press play. She nodded and on the press of a button, the blurry colourless images on the screen sprang into action.

The scene was set; the empty bar they'd been in earlier was filled with extras going about their social business. Jack was behind the bar serving drinks with another member of staff. Just as he had suggested, Joseph Warren and Ed Braithwaite could be seen sitting on the corner of the bar, pints in hand. Both were similarly dressed in shirts and blazers. Ed was the distinctly larger man of the two, but their features were similar. Pale skin. Tall. Plainly cut hair, which the detectives knew was mousy brown in colour. The difference between the two – though it could not be seen in the colourless tape – was in the eyes. Ed Braithwaite's had been a subtle hazel whilst Joseph's were a striking blue, his irises the colour of a Himalayan poppy, melting into a deep blueberry rim.

In the footage, Ed was talking animatedly to Joseph, when a group of girls, entered and barged into the bar next to them. Ed's back was knocked by one of them, so he turned to look at them. It appeared the tall, skinny, dark-haired woman was very apologetic, though there was no audio, so the detectives could only hazard a guess as to what was being said. The two exchanged a hand-shake. Joseph seemed only to watch them. A round of drinks was ordered. Interestingly, Joseph footed the bill upon receiving a nudge from his friend, who continued talking to the woman who had knocked into him.

Lowe focused her attention on the gaggle of girls.

Aside from the tall brunette engaged with Ed, there were four more: a short one with a bob, another tall dark-featured one, a medium height curly-haired woman and the messy blonde in the floral dress that they knew all too well.

'That's our girl,' Lowe pointed. Her attention would now be split between them. The doctor and Anna. Hayes skimmed forward across more of the tape. Ed had begun talking to Anna, whilst two of the other women swooned over Joseph. He was politely responsive to them, but all the while seemed fixated in the direction of his friend and Anna.

Or at least that was how it appeared to Lowe.

They all quickly consumed more alcohol, all except Joseph, who drank at a steady pace. Ed had been drinking heavily. If, as Joseph had suggested, he'd driven home, he was way over the limit. The corpse was not entirely innocent. However, that observation was pointless now. He was dead, and none of what happened had occurred in a car accident. The car had already been located and sent for analysis. It was the only evidence they'd had back so far. It seemed odd that it was processed first, before the immediate crime scene. Perhaps it was because of the size. No traces of blood or anything suspicious had been found in the car, just Anna's belongings, which had helped them to ID her in the first place.

As the timecode read twenty-two: seventeen: thirty-two Joseph stood up from his chair and Ed put his jacket back on. They were getting ready to leave, at around the time Joseph had truthfully recounted. Anna too picked up her small bag from the bar.

Lowe and Hayes leaned in.

Ed motioned to the door whilst in chat with some of the girls. Three of them shook their heads whilst saying indistinguishably fast sentences. The short one with the bob latched her arms around Joseph. He awkwardly removed himself from her grasp. The unidentified tall brunette, Anna, Ed and Joseph walked away from the bar, in the direction of the exit.

Hayes switched the camera view to the one outside of the bar.

The foursome came through the doors of the exit, passed the security guard and seemed to stand chatting outside, the two women facing the two men. The tall brunette stumbled around a little talking on the phone. Minutes later, a car pulled up. She kissed Anna on the cheek and got into the car, which pulled away. Ed motioned to Anna to follow him towards his vehicle. She declined, waving her hand in front of her and shaking her head. Her phone was in her other hand. At that moment, Joseph outstretched his arm and placed his palm on Anna's back, smiling. She was then ushered in the direction of the car and the trio disappeared off into the right of the screen.

The tape finished. Neither Lowe or Hayes said anything.

'Well, that's open to interpretation…' Tabbot's voice startled them. They looked up to see he was leaning in the doorway, arms folded, facing the screen. They didn't know how long he'd been there or what he'd watched as they'd been so focused on the footage.

'Sure is, doesn't really tell us much. Only confirms Anna Miller left with both men,' Hayes agreed.

'The lawyers will have fun with that as evidence,' Tabbot commented, before adding, 'supports Warren's story so far...'

Hayes turned to Lowe, wondering how his colleague would react to the footage and Tabbot's comments.

'Mm,' she nodded in apparent agreement.

'Get an ID and interview those lasses,' Tabbot instructed nonchalantly, before leaving to go about his business. Lowe turned to Hayes.

'You want to go and get that ball rolling?' she asked.

'Yep, on it.' He stood up, gathering his notes and left the room. Lowe watched him as he walked out, waiting for him to close the door.

Once he was out of sight, she snatched up the remote and rewound the tape. Once again, she watched as the four exited the bar and the brunette left in the car that pulled up. She watched Ed indicate to what she assumed was his own vehicle. She watched as Anna shook her head and noticed this time that she had also put a foot back...she was going to find an alternative route home. She watched the very moment where, just as Anna was taking that step back, Joseph's arm reached up towards her back and a smile spread across his lips.

Lowe paused the tape and looked at the still image in front of her: the hand on Anna's back and the sickening, deceptive smirk on Joseph Warren's face. The moment perhaps, that would lead to the events that happened in that basement bedroom that night. Lowe was sure she detected a hint of discomfort in the wide-open eyes of Anna Miller.

The Friends

On Tabbot's orders, Lowe had prioritised interviewing the women from the bar over appealing for neighbourhood witnesses. It hadn't taken long for them to go over receipts and track down the names of the four women. Once they'd found one, they'd managed to find them all.

The first to be identified and tracked was the curly-haired woman called Talia Burgess. Talia was the first one interviewed and led to them to the other three: Elle Mason, the short blonde with the bob and the two tall dark-featured women, Olivia Harding and Courtney Woods, the one who had bumped into Ed in the first place. Other than this, Talia hadn't offered much more to the investigation. She was just a friend of Elle's who had tagged along and only met Anna that night. Olivia had unfortunately travelled north to be with her terminally ill mother and so they were unable to pull her in for questioning. Luckily, they had been able to reach the remaining two.

Lowe and Hayes split up the interviews of the two remaining women between them. Hayes entered one of the interview rooms and greeted Elle with a standard handshake.

'Hi Elle, thank you for coming in. I'm sure you're aware of why you're here?'

'Yes, I heard what happened. I can't believe it.'

'Can I get you anything before we start? Tea? Water? Something to eat?'

'Actually, a cup of tea would be great, if it's not too much trouble?'

'Not at all, one moment.' Hayes left the room to ask an administrator to bring a cup of tea, who did so promptly. Once settled, Hayes sat down to face Elle, placing his files on the table in front of him and handing Elle the tea in a tacky polystyrene cup. She thanked him for it and he pressed play on the tape recorder.

'Before we start, would mind stating your name for the tape?'

***

In an adjoining interview room, Lowe entered with two cups of water and a file tucked under her arm. She placed one cup in front of the interviewee and another on her side of the table. She sat down.

'Hi, Courtney Woods?' Lowe began, opening the file.

'Yeah, that's me,' the woman spoke with an unexpectedly high-pitched Essex accent.

'Miss Woods, I'm DCI Abigail Lowe. Thanks for agreeing to meet with me,' Lowe introduced herself, flicking over the list of questions they'd prepared for the witnesses.

'This about Anna Miller?' Courtney asked. Lowe looked up to meet the woman's eyes. 'Shame what 'appened to the Doctor, ain't it?'

Lowe closed the file and leaned forward placing her elbows on the table and clasping her hands. 'And why do you say that?' She tilted her head to one side, awaiting an answer.

'Well, 'e's a nice man ain't he? He was sure nice at the bar. Both of 'em were. And I know Anna, she's a nut job. She'll do anythin' for a story, her.'

'Can you confirm for me how you know Anna?'

'Yeah, we work togeva.'

'Right, and what story do you think she was after, exactly?'

'I dunno, probably one abou' the doctor cheating on his wife wiv her. She got a lot of debts to pay off from her journalism course ennit, so she can sell a story, she gets some cash. Then she can pay it off.'

'Right. Can you give me one moment please Miss Woods?' Lowe asked, getting up from her chair and exiting the room. She walked down the corridor and knocked on the door where Hayes was interviewing Elle Mason and went in.

'Sorry to interrupt,' she nodded to the witness before turning to Hayes, 'can I borrow you for a sec?'

Hayes excused himself from the interview momentarily, leaving the room with Lowe, pulling the door to behind him.

'What is it, what's up?'

'I need you to find out about the relationship between Anna Miller and Courtney Woods, and if you can about any debts Anna might have.'

'Right, sure… will do.'

'Great thanks,' Lowe tapped Hayes on the arm thanking him, before returning to her own interview.

***

'Sorry about that,' Lowe sat back in the chair opposite Courtney. 'Right, can you tell me what happened on the evening of the twenty-fourth when you went to the bar?'

'Yeah, we went out for drinks wiv der girls and we went to Zero cos it's close to the office an' that. There were four of us from work and then one of Elle's friends come too. I forgot 'er name. Anyway, bar was pretty busy an' so we squeezed in to order our drinks, but I bumped inter this guy by accident.'

Lowe took out a photograph of Ed Braithwaite and placed it in front of Courtney. 'Is this the man?'

'Yeah, tha's 'im. Tha's the guy. He was real nice about it, so we got to talking and they bought us a round of drinks. He was with Doctor J. Warren. Course, workin' in media, we recognised him. Pretty cool t' meet him really.'

'Did Anna and Joseph Warren talk at all during the night?'

'Nah, not really. 'e weren't much of a talker. I knew she liked 'im though. She's like that. Always grasping to 'ave the most attention and be the one noticed.'

Lowe watched her. She seemed to speak of Anna with an air of hostility, that Lowe presumed was motivated by jealousy. Either way, it was clear she would have to take this witness statement with a pinch of salt. 'Now, you left with them when they went, didn't you?'

'Yeah, cos my boyfriend was picking me up. He din't wanna come out too late.'

'Did you offer Anna a lift home at all?'

'Nah, she said she was gettin' a taxi.'

'So, you left her alone, with two men you'd just met that night?' Lowe cocked a judgemental eyebrow. Courtney screwed up her face.

'She goes 'ome on her own all the time. The station is in der complete opposite direction to my flat.'

'Right,'

'Besides, she probably wanted t' sleep wiv one of 'em. Which apparently din't go so well for her...' Courtney slumped back in her chair and folded her arms.

'So, to your knowledge, Anna was going to get a taxi home?'

'Yeah. Tha's all I know cos I left then.'

'And did either Joseph Warren or Ed Braithwaite show any interest in Anna Miller?'

'Nah, I mean she's pretty I guess, if yer inter that kinda look, but they din't seem interested. That Ed guy was all over me, but obviously I've got a boyfriend, so that weren't going nowhere. And the doctor's married ennit, so he weren't interested in no one.'

'So, you don't think there was any indication that either of those men would do any harm to your friend?'

'Nah. Not at all. She was the one that 'urt them. Everybody knows that, it's obvious.'

'So, you're saying that you think that your colleague Anna Miller...' Lowe began harshly, pulling out photos taken at the crime scene of Ed Braithwaite's body, '...could do this?'

Courtney swallowed as she looked at the photos with repulsion. She did not answer.

'Hm?' Lowe probed her. 'You think Anna is capable of doing this?'

'Uh...' Courtney didn't know what to say. Seeing the photo had completely thrown her off her mission to condemn Anna.

'Right, I think that's all we need for now. Anything else you'd like to add to before we wrap up?'

The lack of response confirmed to Lowe that Courtney was simply there to bitch about her colleague and wouldn't add anything useful to their investigation, although she'd likely be a good witness to call on for whoever defended Joseph Warren when it came to court. Luckily, thought Lowe, this woman could easily be discredited.

'No? Right then, thank you Miss Woods, my colleagues will show you out,' she said, giving a bitter smile to the witness before picking up the file and leaving the room.

***

In the room down the corridor, Hayes had gone back to interviewing the much calmer Elle, who was sipping her tea when he re-entered.

'Everything OK?' she asked.

'Yeah, yes all fine. Do you mind if I ask you a few questions about the relationship between Anna Miller and Courtney Woods?' He sat back in the chair to face her. She looked a little confused, not seeing the correlation between Courtney and the case. Of course, they were all aware that something had happened that night after Anna had left the bar. She hadn't showed up for work the next day and the papers had reported it as front-page news. It was all over their social media timelines and the news channels. The story was practically inescapable.

'Uh, yeah. Sure.'

'Can you describe their relationship?'

'Uhm, well to be honest with you, it's not great. Like they pretend to get on, because they work together but Courtney doesn't really like Anna. She bitches about her all the time. Personally, I just think she's jealous…'

'What is she jealous about?'

'Pfft… where do you want me to start? I mean, Anna is really good at her job, like really. She won an award last year and it really ticked Courtney off. To confess, we're all a little jealous of how good she is, she manages to find stories like just at the right time, it's crazy. But she also works hard and has two different jobs, she works in a shop on the weekends. She's got a lot of debts to pay back from her courses to be fair. Her parents aren't well off, so she struggled to put herself through school, y'know? I think Courtney has had a lot handed to her, so she thinks she's entitled to all the stuff Anna works hard for.' That answered all of the questions in one go for Hayes and seemed like a valid assessment.

'OK, great. Thanks. Now can you take me through the events of the evening of the twenty-fourth...'

With that question, Hayes heard a version of the events that only supported what was on the CCTV footage and didn't add any indication as to what happened after they left the bar. It did explain Courtney's testimony though, which he later relayed to his partner. The interviews had left them at a dead end and with forensics taking their time due to the sheer volume of incidents, they had little else to do but appeal for more witnesses and wait.

The Children

'Dad!' Grace, the eldest of Joseph and Elizabeth's children, flung her arms around her father. She was, in all outwards appearance, a younger, albeit taller, replica of her mother. She was slender with long blonde hair and an expensive taste in fashion that was indulged by her father. Besides age, what differentiated Grace from her mother was experience.

Whilst Grace exuded a naïve warmth and happiness, she knew there had always been something cold about her mother. Even when she was happy or smiling, Elizabeth's apparent joy seemed unsettling, the kind that almost appeared forced. No amount of material possessions had cured Elizabeth's discontentment over the years.

Even now, as she and her children were picking up her husband and their father upon his discharge from the hospital, there was a withdrawn element to her. This reserved and cautious manner was a trait their son Theo had inherited. Though, of course, this could be ascribed simply to the tribulations of adolescence. He, like his mother, did not rush into his father's arms, but remained at the foot of the roughly made bed.

'We're so glad that you're OK! When Mum phoned I couldn't believe it.' Grace tightened her arms around her father's torso.

'Careful love, it's still a bit sore,' Joseph winced, but in truth did not mind. The comfort of his daughter was just what he needed after the days in hospital. Finishing his embrace with his daughter, Joseph took it upon himself to hobble over to his son and ruffle his intentionally messy hair, much to Theo's annoyance. 'Alright son?' Joseph asked but as the typical teenager, Theo knocked his hand away.

'Fine,' was the short response.

Nothing's changed, thought Joseph, shaking it off as he turned to kiss his wife who was finishing packing his things into a bag. However, as a wife does when she isn't amused with a husband, Elizabeth turned her face, so he only caught her on the cheek. Joseph immediately sensed her distance and became frustrated with her. Right now, under these circumstances, this wasn't helpful to him. He expected nothing but her upmost support during his time of need.

'Elizabeth…' he tried again, touching her arm just fractionally harder than softly.

'Don't,' she warned him, recoiling from his touch. Both children noticed the tension between their parents and shared a knowing exchange. They did not ask. They never did. They knew their mother was inherently angry at their father for something of which she never spoke. Joseph took the hint and turned back to Theo.

'Happy to see your old man back on his feet?' he asked, in the over-enthusiastic tone all parents use to attempt interaction with their kid, who is at that disengaged stage between childhood and adulthood.

'What's gonna happen to that woman?' Theo asked indifferently, slumping down into the chair beside the bed and taking out his mobile phone.

'Uh…' Joseph looked to Elizabeth for help, but she did not look up from folding his clothes into the bag. 'Well, we're going to press charges, she'll be arrested when she wakes up, the police are doing a very good job.'

Theo screwed up his face. 'Isn't is like murder though… what she did to Uncle Ed?'

'Theo!' Elizabeth exclaimed, shooting her son a warning glance.

'What?! It must be, that's what all the people at school are saying, and it makes sense with what Dad's saying too.'

Elizabeth shook her head at her son and returned to packing the bag more ferociously.

'All the papers are saying it too…' Grace added, sitting elegantly on the bed. 'You should see what they're writing online; they're calling her a psychopathic stalker.'

'Well…' Joseph looked again for help from his wife, but once again she did not look up. 'I'm not too sure at the moment, but she'll probably be charged with murder.'

'I'll meet you in the car,' Elizabeth said huffily, grabbing the bag and marching out of the room. Joseph turned to his children.

'Who forgot to give her, her happy pills this morning?'

'She's just upset about Uncle Eddy and you worried her. You scared us all Dad…She'll be OK.' Grace smiled reassuringly. In truth, Grace didn't know this. She only hoped.

***

When Joseph returned home, he was pleased to discover the crime scene had been cleaned up. He couldn't bear to come back to it. The children were both pleased to have him home, even if his wife was not. He too was glad to be home and even a little relieved when Elizabeth told him she was going food shopping, since they had little in and everyone was home now. Grace agreed to go and help her. Which left only Theo in the house with him. This wouldn't be a problem, since Theo spent most of his time in his room playing video games – ever the living stereotype that he was. This gave Joseph the opportunity to do what he really wanted to do.

As soon as he was sure everyone was either out or occupied, he went in search of what he was looking for – starting in the basement bedroom. He went from room to room, pulling open drawers, wardrobes, looking high and low, but he still could not find the one item he was urgently searching for.

'Uh…Dad, what're you doing?' Theo's question startled Joseph. He looked up to see the confused expression veiling his son's features. Joseph straightened himself, shutting the drawer he was looking in.

'Nothing… nothing,' he smiled. Theo looked to him, dubious. 'I was just looking for my phone charger.' This was, of course, a lie. He wasn't looking for his charger at all. He was hunting the one piece of evidence that oh-so-smart detective had let slip she hadn't recovered.

He needed to find it, before someone else did.

The Lead

As Tabbot had requested following the media traction to the case, Lowe and Hayes had finally gotten around to doing house calls to appeal for witnesses in the area. They'd hoped to get some other members of the team to do this part as it was so tedious. Unfortunately, their resources had been limited due to other ongoing investigations, so they had to bite the bullet and do it themselves.

So far, they'd mostly been met with gossipy and opinionated neighbours, who offered nothing significant to the investigation as it stood. It was as if the incident had injected a burst of excitement into their dull and monotonous money-earning lives. Little did any of them actually realise the severity of the situation.

Nothing like this had ever happened in the community and everyone wanted to have their say or offer their piece – especially when it came to the mysterious offender Anna Miller, who was currently comatose and handcuffed to a hospital bed, awaiting arrest when – if – she regained consciousness. So far, the verdict remained: Doctor J. Warren was a saint and what had happened to him and his poor friend was unforgivable. The upper to middle-class had spoken: the harshest punishment possible should be bestowed upon the culprit.

Both detectives were growing restless. Even Hayes was beginning to lose his will to go on with questioning the neighbours. Anticipating an identical conversation to those they'd already had with the residents of the previous houses they'd tried, Lowe and Hayes met in the middle, knocking on the door of the final house.

'More of the same?' Lowe rolled her eyes as they waited for the occupants to answer.

'Pfft. I've never met such a boring and pretentious set of people. I'm with you, this is a complete waste of time,' Hayes complained.

'That may be but, got to make the Super happy!' Lowe sneered, pulling a purposely fake smile as she knocked on the door again.

'Mm, regardless, I still think this is a waste of – ah hello Ma'am.' Hayes was interrupted by the tiny frame of a gaunt older woman opening the door.

'Uh, hello,' the neighbour responded uncertainly, looking between the two, holding the door closely to her.

'I'm DI Ellis Hayes and this is DCI Abigail Lowe,' he flashed her his badge. 'I'm sure you're aware of the events that took place just down the road, we're just asking around the neighbourhood, to see if anyone saw or may know anything that can help us.'

'Who's at the door, Sar?' a man in the background called, appearing beside her and pulling the door open. He too was skinny with mole-prone skin and dark mouse-like eyes.

'These are the detectives working on Joe and Elizabeth's case,' she turned to him timidly.

'Oh, hello, hello, come on in!' The man moved aside with confidence to let them through. They thanked him and went in, where they were led through to a living room practically indistinguishable from the others they'd visited on the street, the garish floral furniture the only obvious difference. They learnt this couple were called John and Sarah Thacker.

'Would you like a cup of tea or anything?' Sarah asked politely.

'Oh, no thank you,' Hayes answered whilst Lowe shook her head and smiled.

'So, how long have you both known the doctor and his wife?' Lowe started.

'We go way back, since Wellington Joe and I, why we simply couldn't believe it when we discovered we lived on the same street! Our kids were all young, ours perhaps a little older, but they grew up together. Fantastic friends, truly good people, a lovely family,' John explained animatedly, his trimmed moustache dancing about on his lips. Great, more of the same thought both detectives.

'Were you–' Lowe started to ask about the evening of the crime but was yet again interrupted by yet another man.

'Terrible what happened I say, truly awful. Has the girl been apprehended yet? I would hope so given what she did. Rotten woman. We've seen her lurking here a few times haven't we Love?' John asked his wife but did not give her the chance to respond. 'Yes, it was unfortunate that Joe ended up getting tricked by her. He is always so nice to his supporters and fans. Oh, and his poor friend Eddy! We hope justice is done. Poor family. Just horrible.'

'Do you have any evidence to support your claim that Miss Miller has been lurking around here?' Lowe queried, quite rightly, noting that his words seemed awfully similar to those quoted in the tabloids.

'I don't stand at the window with a camera!' John screwed up his face, a little offended at being doubted. He couldn't possibly comprehend the obvious and unwarranted distrust from this policewoman coming into his home and asking him for help. His word was always, and should always, be taken at face value. It was clear in her expression that she didn't believe him.

'We just have to be thorough. I'm sure you can understand that. Were you in on the evening of the twenty-fourth?' Hayes offered, turning the man's attention back to himself.

'Of course, I understand. Hmm…were we in on the evening of the twenty-fourth? We were out, were we not Darling?' He turned to his wife again, waiting for her to answer this time.

'No…' she began anxiously, but a darting look from her husband made her change her story, 'I, uh, yes sorry, we were out, visiting our son.'

Unfortunately, both detectives had caught the warning glance from the husband. They'd been trained enough to know that there was probably something more that this couple knew but were not going to share with them.

'You're sure? You didn't see or don't know anything?' Lowe directed her question to Sarah.

'No, we don't know anything,' John cut in. His manner, and treatment of his wife throughout their conversation had really begun to annoy Lowe, and something had made her quite short tempered of late, so Hayes knew that her restraint was not so easy to keep. This man was pushing her.

'Anything at all Mrs Thacker…' she tried again.

'I just told you woman, we don't know anything. We were out.' John continued to answer for Sarah.

'I am asking your wife, please let her speak!' Lowe snapped. John Thacker, a man who evidently wasn't used to being put in his place, was taken aback.

'Excuse me, this is my home. You will not speak to me that way,' he barked crossly.

'All I'm asking is for you to let your wife answer, unless there is some reason why you won't let her?'

'John, it's OK,' Sarah tried.

'No! No, it isn't! *She* cannot speak to me like that.' He was becoming angrier.

'She?' Lowe asked, not appreciating the tone.

'Oh dear, I think it would be best if –' It didn't matter what Sarah said. She was too passive for her words to be registered by the others in the room, least of all by her husband.

'Is she even a real copper or just there to fill the diversity quota?' John shot to Hayes.

Lowe scoffed. The sheer arrogance of this man made her want to physically punch him, an impulse she rarely experienced.

'John! Oh, I'm so sorry…' Sarah shrieked, turning helplessly to Lowe, clearly embarrassed by her husband but too submissive to really stop him.

'I think we'll be leaving now. Thank you for your time.' Hayes took control of the situation and began to usher Lowe out. She composed herself, pulling down the jacket of her black pantsuit, stroking her stomach twice. She took a deep breath. She still wanted to know what the wife was going to say.

'Yes, sorry to take up your time. If you think of anything else, please, give us a call.' Lowe reached into her pocket and held out a contact card to Sarah, which was quickly snatched up by John. She gave him a forced smile and they exited the house.

***

'Do you have to piss off everyone we interview?' Hayes asked, somewhat seriously as they began to walk down the clean, paved street to their car.

'Oh, I'm to blame for that one, am I?' Lowe looked to him in disbelief.

'You are an officer of the law Abbie, you need to keep your cool. That was unprofessional, and you shouldn't have let it escalate.'

'She knew something Ellis!'

'I know!' he raised his voice. Regaining a sense of his surroundings, he sighed and calmed himself, 'I know, but that wasn't the way to go about it. You don't provoke people who can be useful to an investigation. I can't believe I'm saying this to you of all people. I've never seen you like this, you're usually so detached and even a comment like that wouldn't bother you. What's gotten into you?'

Lowe wanted to shout back at Hayes, the anger still flickering inside, but found she couldn't. She knew, deep down, that he was right and that she had let the man get under her skin. She just wanted answers, to find out what really happened in that room on the night of the twenty-fourth, and the fact that this bigoted old man was intentionally obstructing her path made her sick to the core. Lowe was so used to dealing with homicides and victims that were dead, it was easier to not grow attached, but something about Anna Miller, the way they'd found her, something really bothered Lowe about it. What bothered her more, was everyone else's opinion.

Of course, it wasn't impossible that a woman, of a relatively average height and weight, could overpower two large men, and even kill one of them. The trouble was, in her heart Lowe knew that wasn't what happened. It was frustrating that all the evidence and testament so far supported the portrayal of Anna Miller as a criminal. Lowe herself couldn't dispute that Joseph Warren's version of events was credible. She couldn't even pinpoint why she couldn't believe what everyone was saying and was convinced of: that Joseph was innocent, and Anna was guilty.

Ultimately, it wasn't her job to determine this, that would be the job of a jury, but she could not silence the part of her that wanted to act in favour of the young person she'd found lying battered, bruised and bleeding in that basement bedroom.

'I'm sorry,' she stopped as they reached the car and turned to Hayes, giving in.

'It's alright, just keep the lid on in future.'

'I will…' she swore unconvincingly. Hayes cocked an eyebrow at her. 'I will! I promise!' She held her hands up.

Hayes began to unlock the vehicle, but before opening the door he put his hands on the roof of the car and looked her dead in the eye. 'And for what it's worth Abs, he shouldn't have said what he said. That was wrong. I'm sorry he said it,' he spoke sincerely.

She smiled at the honest and good man in front of her. 'Thank you. Really,' she softened, opening the door to get in the passenger seat, but as she did she heard a faint calling from behind.

'Detective Lowe! Hello, excuse me, Detective Lowe!' It was Sarah, the lady they'd just spoken to, walking briskly towards them, still in her slippers. They turned to her.

'Are you OK ma'am?' Hayes asked.

'There was a charge…' Sarah caught her breath. 'Against Joe, about twenty years ago, but it was dropped or something. It disappeared,' she spoke quickly in a low voice. She did not want to be overheard saying something against the cherished member of the community.

'What kind of charge?' Lowe asked, intrigued by the new information. Could this help her prove what she'd initially thought? Had she given in to the pressure from her superior and cleared Joseph's name too early? Was he, as she suspected all along, responsible for what happened in that room?

'I can't say anymore. I have to get back. John'll kill me. Just. Look into it,' she said firmly, with almost pleading eyes, before starting to back away.

'We will. Thank you, thank you!' Lowe smiled reassuringly as the woman nodded and walked away, back to the comfort of her fifties style marriage.

'Well, that's a development…' Hayes said, almost excited.

'That it is. Let's go.'

The Charge

Lowe sat at her desk, under a harsh lamp, searching the police database. Hayes lounged beside her, reading the newspaper as he awaited the results of Lowe's search. They were practically the only two left in the office this late, but the lead was too good not to follow up on immediately.

'I have to say Abs, I am starting to see why Warren gets on your nerves,' Hayes said casually, taking a sip of the coffee he'd made to help them stay awake for the later shift.

'Mm?' Lowe mumbled, only half-listening as she scrolled through searches.

'Yeah, he's already issued his own statement to the press. Playing up to it a little too much. Probably he's making a pretty penny out of selling the story. Morals aren't quite right... bet it's on the news. Hold on.' Hayes hopped up to grab a remote and switched on a mounted flat screen in the background. Skipping through channels, he found that his assumption was indeed correct.

Joseph was stood in front of a hospital entrance, addressing the press, with his family in the background. His statement in the news clip began: "I am deeply affected by what has happened. It is unforgivable."

'Turn it up please,' Lowe looked up from her search. Hayes upped the volume, standing to watch as their assumed victim continued.

"The damage to myself, to my family and the loss of our dear friend and renowned professor Edward Braithwaite is something we cannot easily recover from. We would like to take this time to grieve together as a family and move past this. We will not hesitate to ensure justice comes to the sick and twisted person who murdered Eddy and so freely caused us this pain. At this time, I would ask you to respect my family's privacy. Thank you."

The clip ended with Joseph smiling and waving politely, before walking away with his family. Hayes muted the TV.

'Slightly showy for someone wanting privacy,' he retorted, sitting back down in his chair and leaning back, fiddling with the remote.

'It's only going to make our jobs harder, he's making himself untouchable by controlling the narrative in the media.' Lowe gave Hayes an unamused look, before returning to her search.

'Course, he is a personality, so I guess the statement would make sense,' Hayes tried to find reasoning. Really, he was just trying to keep his mind occupied whilst waiting for Lowe to finish their pursuit of an old charge filed against Joseph Warren.

'Mm,' Lowe agreed, clicking into a file.

'Going to be lots of pressure on us to make an arrest and then on the lawyer they hire to try her. It's going to be a public case. Nasty business,' Hayes mused. Lowe did not reply. He looked to her reading intently and then sat up abruptly. 'What? What is it? What've you found?'

Lowe looked to him, a half-satisfied smirk spreading across her face.

'The neighbour was right. Nineteen years ago.'

'You're kidding?' Hayes leaned over, moving Lowe's untouched coffee, to better see the screen.

'Nineteen years ago. Charges dropped after some kind of settlement with a University. Victim's name is blacked out on the screen. It's been redacted, which is weird. I'll appeal for the original info. But Ellis, I could be right. Look at the charge...'

Hayes looked directly into the box and sure enough, in messy black handwriting, thickened by the photocopy that digitised the file, the charge was written: sexual assault.

The *Wife*

The next day, following their discovery of the former charge against Joseph, the detectives knocked on the black door of number twenty-nine again. The disappointment on Elizabeth's face when she opened the door and saw them foreshadowed how the encounter would go.

'Hi, we're here to talk to your husband again if that's OK Mrs Warren? Is he in?'

'No. He's out. Attending a memorial for Eddy at Imperial with my daughter.'

'Do you have any idea what time he'll be back?' Hayes asked.

'No.'

'Mrs Warren, we've come across a charge against your husband nineteen years ago. Given the circumstances in which Anna Miller was found, we'd really like to ask him some questions,' Lowe was firm. Elizabeth stared at her for a moment, astounded.

'He not home. I told you,' she persisted, but this time there was a hint of apprehension in her voice.

'We'd rather not discuss this on the street...' Hayes began but Elizabeth's abrupt tongue cut him off.

'My son is here! I think you should leave,' she spat, beginning to close the door on them. Lowe picked up on the defensive change in Elizabeth's behaviour, but her own determination to discover the truth forced her to ignore it. She stuck her hand on the door to prevent it from closing.

'Mrs Warren, do you know anything about the former sexual assault charge filed against your husband?' Lowe inquired bluntly.

'Mum?' a young adolescent voice called from behind.

Lowe looked up to see the figure of a boy turning into a man. Something innate made her immediately regret her decision to push. She shouldn't have asked that when a child was present. She was out of order. She withdrew her hand. Elizabeth had turned and was in a deep silent exchange with her son.

'Mrs Warren...' Lowe tried, but Hayes put his hand on her upper arm to restrain her. Lowe shook him off gently as Elizabeth turned back to face them, a look of fierce defensiveness directed towards this ignorant detective who had come to her house to heartlessly stir up her family's history.

'I think you need to leave now.' Elizabeth tried to shut the door again.

'Mrs Warren,' Lowe attempted again, this time putting her foot to the door.

'Now!' Elizabeth pushed the door harder.

'Mrs Warren. I'm sorry. I didn't mean to–' Lowe blurted out.

'Please, go,' Elizabeth's eyes begged her. Lowe moved her foot and the door was shut in her face.

***

Inside the house, Elizabeth turned to face her son. His tall, scrawny frame stood tensely as he waited for an explanation from

94

his mother. This was the kind of exchange that no mother should have to have with her child. A deep dredging of the suppressed past. A purposely omitted conversation to protect the future. Now the past that Elizabeth had refused to face, was catching up with her.

'Is it true, what the detective said?' Theo looked at her, willing the truth.

'Theo. I. It's…no.' Elizabeth wasn't sure what to say. Nothing had prepared her for this.

'Mum. Do you know what they were on about?' he persisted, sensing his mother was holding something back.

'I…it's complicated Theo, you, you're too young to understand,' she replied evasively, going to him and reaching out her hands. He recoiled from her.

'No. Tell me. Tell me the truth. What were they talking about?' His voice was harder. He was confused. Upset. Angry. Unsure.

'Theo,' she tried, pain visibly consuming her features.

'Mum.' A firm, impatient response. Elizabeth had no choice. She couldn't lie to her son. She wouldn't, not to protect the man she called her husband.

'It was nothing. Really. It was just a misunderstanding between your dad and I many years ago,' she offered a shortened, ambiguous version.

'He hurt you?' Theo hissed.

Until that point, Theo had not considered that it could have something to do with his mother. Though young, he was not stupid. He could put two and two together very quickly. Elizabeth could only look at him helplessly. She didn't want to relive the events of the past, just as she didn't want to reveal them to her young, innocent son. She didn't want to speak the words out loud. In fact, there was so much stored inside of her that she'd never revealed to anyone. The only person who had known the whole and full truth was Eddy, but he would be taking it to his grave.

'When? What happened?' Theo almost choked on his own anger. In the utterance of a few small words, his world had completely shattered. The man he knew as his father was not the upstanding community icon everyone made him out to be. There was a hidden, dark side of him that only his mother knew. A side his father would only reveal to her.

'It was around twenty years ago...it really was just a misunderstanding. It doesn't matter anymore Theo.' Elizabeth tried to dismiss it but the raw feelings that she'd stifled all those years ago were boiling inside and rising to the surface.

'Does Grace know?'

Elizabeth shook her head manically. 'No. You can't tell her, please Theo, you can't, it would destroy her. I didn't want you to know or find out like this...oh...I'm sorry. I'm so, so sorry!' Elizabeth lost all control.

Theo stood looking at his mother. Really looking. And this time seeing. Seeing a side of her he'd never seen before. A vulnerable, broken woman. For the first time, he saw his mother as fragile, as years' worth of fear, hurt, anger, pain, repression and loneliness were releasing themselves at once from her body. She must have been so resilient, and it must have taken a strength he'd never know to hold that inside for so long. To marry the man that hurt her. To bear his children. To be trapped in a lie, all to uphold one man's reputation. Theo didn't know how he would be able to face his father again.

It was in that exact moment, standing in the hallway watching his mother break, that Theo grew up.

Shocked and unsettled though he was, this wasn't about him. This was about her. This was his mother. This was a woman who needed help. Without thinking he took her into his long, gangly arms, clutching her tightly. He wanted her to know she was safe. Whatever damage his father had caused, he would help her heal – whatever way she needed. She would not be alone again. He was there.

'Mum… did he hurt that woman in the hospital?' It was the last question Theo needed answered. Elizabeth's only response was to tighten her arms further around her son, but that said it all.

The Last Chance

Lowe had messed up. She never should have bombarded Elizabeth like that. She felt horrible. Guilty. Annoyed at herself. She just needed something, anything, to make her feel better.

Without thinking, she'd driven back to the only place she knew where to go. The only place she really shouldn't go.

'Hi,' she bit her lip as the door opened on her. Rob took a deep breath, moving aside to let her in. She walked into the hallway, standing close, facing him as he closed the door.

'Hi,' he replied unmoving. She moved in pressing her body against his, wrapping her arms around his neck and taking his face to hers. She kissed him, hard.

Seconds later, he was kissing her too, allowing her to walk over him again. As she began to move with him towards the bed, he knew he couldn't let this happen, not without knowing her answer.

He had to stop before it was too late. He had to know now. He pulled his lips away from hers. Their breath heavy, he put his forehead to hers.

'Are you gonna stay?' he exhaled softly.

As her face dropped and her hands fell to his chest, he knew the answer. He pushed her away gently at the waist and let her go. He couldn't look her in the eye anymore. He turned away from her, releasing the frustration he was feeling. Lowe watched the back of him, her mouth slightly open but unable to form words.

'I can't do this,' he said, finally facing her.

'What?' she frowned. It was just sex. It wasn't exactly difficult. He was even good at it, or at least, he satisfied her needs.

'This. Whatever this…is. I just. I want more Abs,' he looked at her, wishing that she would finally tell him what he longed to hear. She looked down. She couldn't give him what he wanted.

'I can't,' she told him, standing sorrowfully on the spot. He went to her, taking her hands and holding them in his.

'How do you know? You could give us a shot. I love you Abs, you know I do. For some fucked up reason. Isn't that worth anything?' he pleaded with her. She snatched her hands back and sighed.

She knew in her heart that he did love her, it wasn't the first time they'd had this conversation. No matter how much he wanted her to, she couldn't feel the same way. She shouldn't have let it come to this. She should have put a stop to it a long time ago, when she first knew he was beginning to feel something for her. She shouldn't have let it go this far, but she couldn't help herself. Whatever it was that she craved every time things got rough, he somehow fulfilled it. That was all. He was just a means to an end. Now, she would have to let him down – again.

'I'm sorry.' Her eyes flickered up to his.

'Then we're done. No more.' Rob closed his soulful brown eyes in pain and walked away from her. He meant it.

'Rob…'

'No. This is over Abigail. Whatever this fucked up thing is. It's over. You can't just come here anymore and use me whenever you need a pick me up and then ignore me for days on end. You can't come here anymore. I'm done. Go and get your kicks somewhere else, pick someone up in a bar. I'm sure every bloke there is just looking for a woman who's easy and up for a fuck.'

He was angry and projecting. As he finished his outburst, he caught a glimpse of her face. He had offended her.

'Shit, Abbie... that's not what I meant.'

But it was too late. Lowe tightened her lips and stormed out of his apartment, slamming the door behind her. She didn't need him, and she certainly didn't need to be insulted by a man who had only just chosen to stand up for what he wanted, after two years.

She left him standing guiltily, angrily, upset and heartbroken in his lonely apartment.

The *Woman*

The immediate burst of light scorched Anna's pupils. Squinting several times to adjust to the light and regain a focused vision, she finally opened her eyes.

The ceiling was plain, simple and boring, made of those sickly tiles that could easily be taken out and crumbled. The walls were a pale colour, probably a faded blue. The corners of the room were sharp and miserable. Multi-coloured pom-poms on stalks sat in a vase on a cabinet with scattered square cards. The scent of disinfectant lingered around the room, but all Anna could smell was the dry tubes blocking her nose, which she soon realised was itchy.

She followed the grey cables running from the blue and red sticky pads on her chest, all the way up to the monitors, the small and miserable beeping robots charting signs of life. Plastic hung on a rusting silver stand, with transparent fluids dripping into similarly clear tubes, that in turn filtered into the sharp needle stabbing into her stiffened, dry hand. A loose white robe with a dizzying green pattern covered the most part of her body, with thin, pale blue sheets slightly warming the rest. Anna was lying as still as stone on a stale, uncomfortable hospital bed.

Looking down towards her cannula infested right arm, Anna began to twitch her fingers. She winced as each one cracked sending ounces of pain shooting upwards. As the tingling fizz settled in her right-hand muscles, Anna slowly turned her stiff neck to conquer the left. Trailing down from her shoulder, over her elbow and along her forearm, her gaze stopped abruptly. Her freedom was snatched at the wrist.

'What?' she exhaled croakily. Then, an instant animal response kicked in and she immediately began yanking at her arm and attempted to squeeze her dainty dry hands through the metal cuff that prisoned her to the hospital bed.

Simultaneously, her frantic activity garnered the attention of the surrounding machinery. Beep. Beep. Beep. Beep. Beep. BEEP. BEEP! The louder and faster the robots screamed, the quicker the faceless blue nurses approached.

'Miss Miller, Miss Miller, please calm – Miss Miller!' An older nurse bearing the name badge Sue, with features as downtrodden as the healthcare system in this country, fought to calm Anna down and restrain her.

'Get this off, let me go!' she spat vehemently.

'It's alright,' Sue assured Anna, before turning to her younger colleague, 'Go and get the doctor please Drew…and call the station.' She added a look indicating he should hurry.

Dutifully, the junior scurried off in search of the ward doctor and to call the detectives that had been pacing around Anna's hospital bed waiting for her to come out of her coma.

'Miss Miller please, calm yourself down or I'll have to do it myself!' Sue warned the young woman struggling on the bed. In truth, the nurse was worried the patient would injure herself further. She had been through quite enough.

She'd come in as an emergency and a whole team of doctors and nurses had worked tirelessly to keep her alive and stable. She'd lost around 3 pints of blood, had a fractured skull (which miraculously didn't have any major bleeds or problems on the brain), she'd had scissors stuck into her pelvis that had torn through a number of internal structures, a dislocated shoulder, a few other deep cuts, an incredibly low heart rate and pretty bad bruising over her body.

She'd had to undergo surgery from the scissor damage, which would severely limit her chances of having children in the future. Breaking this news to her would be yet another trauma on top of whatever she'd already been through. The medical team probably would have felt sorry for her, had they not all been aware that she was a prime suspect in the Doctor J. Warren case.

Most of them knew the doctor well. He was a great man, a respected one and practically a medical genius. He'd never hurt a fly. He'd dedicated his whole career to saving lives and helping people. Her: a journalist that attacked a man when she couldn't get a story from him. Whilst her recovery would take some further time, they were assured in knowing that as soon as she was healthy enough she would be arrested, and justice would be served.

The combined pain she was causing herself and the nurse's warning made Anna give in and settle.

'What...' she tried but was so gravelly, she almost choked on the dryness of her throat. Sue immediately brought some water to the patient's lips, which she took willingly and fast.

'What happened, how did I get here?' she managed to get out finally. The nurse swallowed as she put the water back on the table. This kind of stuff was, quite frankly, way above her paygrade.

'Um, the doctor will be along to explain everything in a moment. You've been through quite a lot, so it's best if you stay here calmly and rest,' Sue said tactfully. Anna looked down at the handcuffs again, noting it wasn't as if she had a choice but to stay put.

'What day is it?' she asked, trying to recollect her thoughts and memories which were darting about all over the place inside her head.

'It's the ninth of November, Friday,' Sue told her. She'd been unconscious for just over two weeks, just lying there, desperate to be able to move, talk, reach out and tell someone what had happened to her. Though she'd tried, only her brain kept on churning whilst her body remained paralysed.

The questions now were: what did she remember, how much did she remember and what would her side of the story be?

'Ah, welcome back Miss Miller,' the ward doctor entered cheerfully. She took one look at the man in front of her, his tall frame, neat haircut and sharp blue eyes. He looked the spit of the man who had hurt her. She stared, wildly afraid of him, her pulse racing, her breathing becoming erratic, her body violently shaking. Yet she did not speak. She just continued to stare, shaking her head as tears dashed out of their ducts.

As the beeping returned to a worrying state, the ward doctor turned to Sue for an explanation, but she had none to offer. The patient had been steady and OK, all things considered, just moments ago, before he had entered. She was responsive and engaging with Sue and her heart rate had steadied. It did not take the ward doctor long to deduce that his presence in the room may be the causing factor of this reaction.

He, unlike the nurses, had been given a lot more information by the police. Right at the start, when she was brought in, an officer had received instructions asking him to perform a sexual offense evidence collection kit. However, after attending to the more urgent medical issues, he'd later received an update from a superintendent

– one Mark Tabbot – telling them to forget this as it would not be relevant to the case.

Yet, Anna's reaction to him, a male doctor, with similar features to the man they all knew was involved in the incident, may have indicated this decision had perhaps been premature. Either way, it was too late now.

The ward doctor called Sue outside.

'I'll get Judith to come and speak to the patient when she gets in, first thing in the morning. I also need you, please, to ensure that it's the female detective that comes into her room. Not the male for now... I don't want to make her situation worse.'

'Are you saying what I think you're saying?' Sue asked knowingly.

The doctor looked into Anna's room before turning and nodding in response to Sue. 'I think so.'

'But Doctor Warren would never...'

'Respectfully Sue, this isn't the first time I've seen a woman in hospital on account of that man,' the ward doctor retorted.

It was clear in his tone that he was not a fan of his famous colleague. Perhaps his dislike for Joseph made it easier for him to believe that the woman was, in fact, not a suspect, but a victim. However, that was his personal perspective and would have no place in the investigation. It was down to the detectives to discover the truth, not him.

He chose to walk away and leave Sue to be taken aback by his comment. He would pass this medical case on. He wasn't going to get involved again. At least, not directly.

The Mistake

Hayes bounced into Lowe's peripheral vision eagerly. Knowing exactly what he was about to say, she cut in first, 'Yes, I heard.'

'And you're not moving…why?' he eyed her suspiciously.

'Super wants to see us…' she turned, groaning in her chair. Tabbot had left a rather blunt email in her inbox that morning scheduling a meeting. She could tell by the tone that it wasn't going to be a meeting she enjoyed.

'You're kidding? What about?' Hayes asked, slouching on the desk beside her, suddenly concerned. She shrugged, collecting the documents she was working on into a file on her desk and rising, ready to face whatever Tabbot was going to throw at her next.

'We'll go to the hospital after this. Come on.' She turned on her heel and walked across the floor to Tabbot's corner office, Hayes following cluelessly behind. She knocked and waited for permission to enter, before doing so. Once inside, they were surprised to see that the Chief Superintendent, Michelle Howard, was also there. This couldn't be good.

'Take a seat,' Tabbot began. Both obliged, sitting opposite their two superiors. Lowe looked between them, awaiting an explanation.

'Hello Detectives, thank you for coming in,' the chief smiled at them, that kind of forced smile you give employees before launching into a disciplinary. Why all the pleasantries? Just skip to the point, thought Lowe.

'Sure,' was Lowe's simple response. Hayes reciprocated the smile, clasping his hands together in his lap nervously.

'This is in relation to the Doctor J. Warren Case. There are some things we need to talk about,' her formal manner appeared sincere. Neither Lowe nor Hayes said anything but waited for her to go on.

'We've received a complaint...'

In her gut, Lowe knew it. She'd seen it coming ever since they'd approached the doctor's wife. That visit hadn't gone according to plan and Lowe felt remorseful over the way she had handled it. All she'd wanted was some more information on the charge, she didn't mean to let it slip at the exact moment the Warrens' son had appeared downstairs. She hadn't meant to put Elizabeth in that position.

Regardless, Lowe had now made her stance on the case clear to the wife. Of course, they were going to want her off of it. They'd rather have fresh eyes who weren't so bias against the husband.

'Look, it was my fault. When we visited the wife—' She leaned forward, ready to explain. She was prepared to take the fall for this. It was nothing to do with Hayes.

'Wait. What did you do to the wife?' Tabbot cut in. Lowe looked between the people in the room, realising quickly that this had nothing to do with Elizabeth Warren.

'No. Nothing...what's this about?' she settled back into her chair.

'The complaint was from one of the neighbours that you both spoke to earlier this week. He was unhappy with your conduct,' Chief Howard continued, finally explaining.

It was Hayes who exhaled a laugh before Lowe could respond. All eyes were on him.

'Would this be a John Thacker?' he asked. Chief Howard nodded. Hayes leaned forward, resting his elbows on the desk between them. 'That man has some nerve,' he spat.

'Detective Inspector Hayes,' Chief Howard warned, but he didn't care.

'No. No. It should be Lowe filing a complaint against him! Who does he think he is? He's no right. You know he made offensive and discriminative remarks towards her?'

'Is this true?' Chief Howard asked as both she and Tabbot turned to Lowe.

The conversation in the room had escalated suddenly and Lowe found herself a little overwhelmed. 'Uh…' she looked between the chief, Tabbot and Hayes.

'Yes. It's true. I was there. He should be the one looked into…and if you even think about taking her off the case over that, you are out of your bloody mind!' Hayes stood up, ranting.

Lowe had never seen him so irate. She was flattered that this was in her defence, but for once, she was the one conscious of their position. He couldn't fly off the handle to the chief and super. It would not help their situation at all. She knew how these things went.

'Hayes, Ellis, it's OK,' Lowe tried to assure him, reaching out a hand to pull him back to his seat, before turning to her bosses. 'Really, it's nothing. I'm fine. Please, Ellis, sit down.'

'You're sure? We take these things very seriously DCI Lowe…' the chief superintendent offered her genuine concern. Hayes finally sat back down.

'Ma'am, with respect, there are always going to be people consumed by hate for no reason. Reacting helps only to fuel it. I wish to pursue it no further. Thank you,' Lowe was firm. The comment truly hadn't bothered her. She had grown up in London, it wasn't like it was the first time she'd had such an encounter. She knew, for every obliviously belligerent person, there were thousands of good ones. She'd always chosen to ignore it. She wasn't going to let someone like John Thacker make her believe she was the problem. She wasn't.

'OK,' Chief Howard acknowledged, 'we'll handle the complaint.'

Lowe nodded thankfully. She'd have to thank Hayes later. This meeting could have gone very differently if it weren't for him.

'Will that be all?' she looked between her superiors, ready to leave as she was eager to get to the hospital to see Anna Miller, who had awoken in the early hours of the morning. Their hesitant response indicated that it was not.

'What else?' Lowe sat back in her chair.

Chief Howard coughed and looked to Tabbot, awaiting some planned interaction. It became clear to the detectives that aside from the complaint, they weren't the ones in trouble, Tabbot was.

'It appears I owe you an apology...' he began through gritted teeth. Again, why people never just got to the point annoyed Lowe. Why must she dig in every conversation to find out what people were actually trying to say? Why couldn't they just say it? It would make life a lot easier for a lot of people.

'For?' Hayes chimed in.

Tabbot reluctantly handed over a file to Lowe. She took it, opening it briskly. Hayes looked over her shoulder. The file contained an anonymous tip on the case. One that clearly supported Lowe's original version of events. One that suggested Joseph Warren was the guilty party and one that insinuated that Anna Miller wasn't the first woman to be injured at his hands.

'What...When...Who?' Lowe struggled to form a sentence, taking in all the information.

'We don't know. We fear that, as this is anonymous, the source may also have found their way to the media. There's going to be a lot of eyes on this. It's going to blow up. As in the past, we're expecting more of these,' the chief signalled to the tip, 'we're going to set up a tip-line, some lower level officers and administrators are going to run it for you, whoever's available. You should be pleased DCI Lowe, it supports your initial assessment.

'Evidence analysis is now on high priority, you should get results within a day or so. Now, we're going to support you in finding the evidence, but I need you both to remember, that we're not only looking at the presumed sexual assault of Anna Miller, but also the murder of Edward Braithwaite. I need evidence for both in order to bring charges and make an arrest. We can't risk any action without solid evidence, not with the media watching. Do you understand?' Chief Howard spoke quickly. How the tables had turned. The suspect the victim and the victim the suspect.

'Uh, wow. OK,' Lowe smiled excitedly. 'Thank you, Ma'am.'

'And anything you need, you let me know,' she finished.

Lowe racked through her brain to think of anything she needed. She now had the resource and support to prove what she'd known all along.

'Actually, we're still waiting on the results from the SOEC kit we ordered on Anna Miller when she was admitted to hospital. It's quite unusual, we haven't had anything back yet.'

Chief Howard looked to Tabbot, deeply agitated. He looked down nervously, muttering out his next sentence which would ignite a visceral rage in Lowe.

'I cancelled it. I didn't see any cause at the time to suspect sexual assault and they aren't cheap. I made a mistake.' His confession shot fury through her veins. How could he?

Lowe rose up out of her chair, seething and excused herself. She rushed out of the office, down the stairs, violently pushing open the glass front doors of the station until she could feel the air enter her lungs. She stood, breathing heavily for a moment before the sickening feeling in her stomach caught up with her. She threw up onto the grey gravel beneath her.

The Victim

Determined now even more so than before, to find proof to shut that monster, who walked as a celebrated hero, away in a cell, Lowe entered the hospital with her partner. She was storming so quickly through the corridors, that Hayes had some trouble keeping up. That was until she reached Anna Miller's room. Inside, the woman she'd found injured on the bed, was now conscious and recovering.

Instead of simply opening the door and walking in, Lowe stopped outside the room and peered in through the gaps in the blind behind the window. An older woman, presumably her mother, was talking animatedly to Anna, though Anna herself appeared disinterested. She was still immobile and riddled with cables and tubes, but she was now propped up on the hospital bed, exhaustedly staring into space. Lowe didn't want to begin to imagine what was going through her mind.

Hayes caught up with Lowe at the window and followed her gaze to Anna.

'They've removed the cuffs,' he attempted to start conversation. Lowe said nothing. After a moment's pause, he tried again, trying to make sense of his partner's intense reaction to the case, 'She's had an effect on you huh?'

'It's funny,' Lowe mused, still looking into Anna's hospital room. 'I've dealt with so many homicides involving rape or sexual assault...' she turned fully towards Hayes, a distressed and helpless expression on her face, '...but they've always been the corpse.'

'Right?'

'I don't know, it's stupid... I feel responsible. We're here to serve and protect... and I mean, look at her! How do you come back from something like this Hayes?'

Lowe turned back to watching the young woman lost in her thoughts. She was only twenty-five and had her whole life ahead of her. At least she did have. Who knew what her life would hold now? All they knew for certain was that it wouldn't be the same.

'Abbie, it's... it's not your fault,' Hayes looked at her sympathetically. She looked down, contemplating for a second and when she looked up, he could see that she was unconvinced by his words.

'I feel responsible for putting away that man for what he did to her... as a woman, in my position, you have to understand. I can't let him get away with this. I just... can't.' She brushed her hair away from her forehead and took a deep breath.

Hayes looked at his colleague, her recent inexplicable frustration suddenly becoming clear to him. Nobody had been there to help Lowe when she needed it all those years ago. Her position now made her feel desperately obliged to help another woman in a time of need. Her frustration was in the system that made it so difficult for her to do so.

It was a system that seemed to place everything against proving the circumstances that were so obviously true, because there is little physical evidence to support it (physical evidence mind, that for sexual assault cases could often only practically be recovered immediately after the event). It was a system where words were not enough, where the memories and experiences of these women meant nothing. They were nothing but claims; ephemeral and circumstantial evidence that could so easily be misconstrued or discredited by hard-nosed lawyers, who so willingly ripped apart the victim, right down to the clothing the individual wore which undoubtedly meant they brought their fate upon themselves.

It was a system that punished victims with decades old standard operating procedures. A system that, whatever way you looked at it, allowed celebrated white men to practically walk free, without any consequences or culpability for the horrific, life-destroying crimes they committed.

To stop that happening to Anna, Lowe needed solid, indisputable evidence. The problem was, in a case like this, it was not easy to come by. It was hard. Really hard. Especially with Tabbot's mistake. There was now a chance they wouldn't ever find it. Still, Lowe felt responsible, she couldn't let the burden of proof fall to this traumatised young woman.

'Whatever it is, we'll find it.' Hayes put a supportive hand on his partner's shoulder. She rested her own hand on his, grateful for the support. 'You ready?' he asked her.

'Yeah,' Lowe inhaled.

'Good Luck! SOIT is down the corridor if you need her, think it's Em. Uh, remember, you are here in the capacity of Ed Braithwaite's death too, OK?' Hayes reminded her. She nodded to him as he walked away to grab coffee whilst she spoke with Anna Miller. He would not be sitting in on this one, for obvious reasons.

With that, Lowe finally entered the room. The mother stopped mid-sentence to look up at the detective. Anna did not.

'Uh… hi.' Lowe smiled to the mother briefly before turning to the person she'd been waiting to speak to. 'Miss Miller, I'm Detective Chief Inspector Abigail Lowe…'

114

No response.

'I'm here investigating the death of Edward Braithwaite...' Lowe edged closer. Anna's eyes flickered in her direction momentarily, but then she was gone again. 'I...I...' Lowe looked once more between Anna and her mother nervously, '...I believe I know what happened.'

Finally, Anna's head shot towards Lowe and her eyes fixed on the detective, her pain yearning to escape. This was a positive response, Lowe knew so. She released the breath she was holding in and took another step closer to Anna.

'I want to talk to you about what happened that night,' she continued, consciously aware of Anna's mother in her naturally protective stance, uncertain of this approaching stranger's intentions.

'I'm sorry Detective Inspector, uh Lowe was it. I don't think my daughter is up to questioning. We've already spoken to a uhm, Emily, the officer...' the mother stepped into the space between her daughter and the detective.

Lowe swallowed and put her hand to her stomach. She needed to talk to Anna. She looked to the victim, aching for her to know she was on her side. Anna met her eyes. The sudden stillness in the room contrasted everything that was being said between the two women in this time-stopping, silent exchange.

'It's OK,' Anna said resolutely, turning to her mother. Lowe waited for her to leave the room, but she lingered hesitantly. 'Mum, it's OK,' Anna repeated, indicating for her to let them be alone.

'Right. I'll get some tea.' The mother, both reluctant and begrudging, finally left the room.

Now alone, Lowe found she didn't know where to start. Anna waited, watching the cogs turn in the detective's brain.

'Uh...how are you feeling?' Lowe started, realising she'd marched in here without any consideration of strategy or questioning. Anna simply stared at her through deep shadowed eyes. Lowe shuffled uncomfortably on the spot.

'Miss Miller,' Lowe took another deep breath and walked closer to the bed. 'I would like you to take me through your memory of what happened on the evening of Wednesday the twenty-fourth of October, if you are able?'

Anna's face twitched as she turned quickly to face Lowe, the twinge of pain from the sudden movement getting the better of her. Lowe watched the acute ripple of Anna's cheek muscles. The pain was real. Visible. Excruciating. Already, Anna was trying to suppress it.

'I don't remember all of it,' she admitted finally

'That's OK,' Lowe assured her, finally closing the gap between them, 'I need you to tell me what you do remember, that's all. Nothing more. At any point, if you want to stop, we stop. I promise.'

'They're saying such horrible things, I didn't do it, I didn't...' Anna began to shake her head violently from side to side, as tears finally burst from her despairing eyes. 'I didn't do anything. I didn't. I swear. And they keep writing that I did. Everyone thinks I did. I didn't. I didn't do anything, it was him!' Anna scrunched up her hair in her fingers as she cried into the palms of her hands. Lowe's heart broke for her again in that moment, this poor young woman, so utterly destroyed and helpless.

'I know. Miss Miller... Anna?' Sitting on the bed, Lowe reached out and took Anna's hands from her head and looked her directly in the eyes without blinking. 'I know, and I believe you.'

Lowe wouldn't know it, but those last three words meant everything to Anna. She was the first person to say it. The first person to not question or doubt her. The first person to not try and assign her the blame. The first person who had come here to listen.

116

The first person to know. The first person to finally give Anna the release she needed.

As Anna began to calm under the grasp of the detective, the nurse, Sue, busied herself with a cart outside the room.

The Twenty-Fourth

'Can you tell me what happened on the evening of the twenty-fourth?' Lowe asked. She'd spent some time allowing Anna to compose herself and explained to her what was going to happen. She'd also given herself a chance to think more clearly about the questions she wanted to ask her.

Lowe was now sat on the only chair in the room, facing Anna, who remained in the bed covered by white sheets and knitted blue blankets. Though a bag beside her was open, revealing clothes and toiletries, Anna wore only the hospital-issued gown. Her hair was greasy and clearly hadn't been brushed in weeks. Stitches were mending the wound on her head. Her face appeared gaunt and grey. Her eyes had sunken deeply into her skull, and were lined with red, as if they themselves were bleeding the anguish she was feeling. Bruises were scattered across her arms, many from the incident, some from the multiple cannulas and blood tests she'd incurred. Though hidden, the scars from her surgery were beginning to set on her lower abdomen.

'It's...uhm... a little blurry,' Anna confessed.

'Whatever you remember,' Lowe encouraged. Anna took a deep breath and closed her eyes, inhaling.

118

'We were in the bar…' she exhaled. 'I was with my colleagues.'

'Do you remember which ones?' Lowe requested, though she already knew. They'd mostly all been interviewed but had offered little to no help with the investigation. One had been unavailable. Two had suggested the events were awful, but that Anna was such a lovely person and what the media were saying didn't make any sense, she'd never hurt a fly. Of course, they had all known who Doctor J. Warren was and were – or in most of their cases – used to be, big fans. How could you not idolise of a man who works thirty-six hours straight saving human lives?

Interestingly, the tall brunette who had left with them, Courtney Woods appeared to feel nothing but contempt for her colleague. Either way, they were all witnesses that would no doubt be easily manipulated by lawyers who took on the case after the investigation concluded and charges were made.

Lowe listened as Anna listed her colleagues as accurately as they'd identified them.

'What happened when you got to the bar?'

'Um. Courtney knocked into a man at the bar.'

'Did you recognise the man at the bar?' Anna looked down, thinking. She shook her head.

'What about Joseph Warren, did you recognise him?' Lowe watched her. Anna looked up to meet the detective's eyes. Slowly, she nodded. Lowe continued, 'Had you met him, or had any kind of contact with him at any point before that evening?'

Anna shook her head violently. 'No, but he's well-known. On TV. I'm a journalist. It's my job to know. I recognised his face,' she explained.

Lowe nodded in acknowledgement. 'So, after your friend knocked into the man at the bar, what happened?'

'I don't know, we spoke to them. They bought us drinks.'

'How many drinks did you have?'

'I don't know,' she let out as her eyes flickered guiltily away from Lowe.

'That's OK,' Lowe smiled reassuringly. 'Did you talk to the men at the bar?'

Anna nodded.

'OK, do you remember what you spoke about?'

She thought for a moment. The frustrating lack of vivid memory of the night was obvious and came through in her tone. 'No. I don't know. Maybe about my job. I don't know. I'm sorry.'

'It's OK. Just whatever you remember. Take your time.'

'Courtney was getting along with the other man. I don't remember his name. He seemed nice...oh...' She froze as images flashed into her mind. The hammer. The hits. The blood. She leaned forward slightly, urgently seeking answers, '...he...is he...?'

'I'm afraid so,' Lowe informed her.

Anna sank back into the hospital bed. 'Oh,' she released an unsteady breath and seemed to be drawn back into her thoughts.

'What do you remember about him?' Lowe prompted.

'He tried to help...' Anna tore at the dry skin on her lip.

'Help?'

'Me.' Again she was pulled back into that room, trying to recollect her memories into a clear chronological order.

Lowe gave her a moment, before probing for further information. 'What happened when you left bar?'

'I wanted to go home...'

'...but you didn't?'

'No?'

'Where did you go? Do you remember where you went?'

'In the back of a house.'

'Did you know whose house you were at?'

120

Anna shook her head. She'd never even been to that part of town, let alone that house. As an under-paid junior journalist for a mid-range magazine, she was still living with her parents in her childhood home on the outskirts of the capital, within easy commutable distance for work.

'Do you know how you got to the house?'

'Car. Their car. I wanted to get a taxi, but they kept insisting I go with them... I shouldn't have done that. I should've just gotten a taxi. They just kept saying the station was on their way. I don't really like to argue, and they seemed fine. I just went. I didn't think...'

'So, you got into the car willingly?'

'Yeah,' Anna exhaled. It was occurring to her how naïve she'd been. She should have gotten into a taxi. If she had, she would have been safe...but who is to say if it hadn't been her, it wouldn't have been someone else?

'Do you remember why you went into the house?'

'Oh God...'

'Oh God what?'

'I just... it's all my fault...I...I needed the toilet.' Tears welled up in her eyes. 'I can't believe I was so stupid!' she cried.

'It's OK...It's OK,' Lowe reassured Anna, trying to ignore the effect the girl's discomfort was having on her. 'Just, in your own time, tell me what happened when you were inside the house. Do you think you can do that?'

'Yeah,' Anna nodded with the whole upper half of her body, before taking a moment and starting up again. 'Uh...the doctor showed me to a small bathroom. I went to the toilet. Then when I came out he was standing in the doorway. He was blocking most of it, which was weird, so I tried, I tried to squeeze past him, but then... then he. He. He.' Anna began to choke on her sentence as intense fear sprang to her throat. She threw her head in her hands, embarrassed by her crying but unable to control it. 'I'm sorry. I can't. I'm sorry,' her wet, mumbled apologies came through intermittent weeps.

Lowe shuffled uncomfortably in her seat, small tears welling up in her own sympathetic eyes. She stifled them and swallowed. She hated that she was the one making Anna relive the events of that night.

'We can take a break now, if you'd like?' Lowe offered. Anna shook her head, wiping the still flowing tears from her cheeks. Lowe stood up, ready to stop the recorder on the table.

'No,' Anna sniffed. 'No. I can do it.'

Lowe sat back down and waited for Anna as she composed herself to continue her statement.

'So, when I tried to get around him, he grabbed me and pushed me into a wall and tried to kiss me,' she sniffed again. 'I tried to push him away, but he was so strong. I asked what he was doing, and he said... eurgh. He said. Mm.'

Anna shut her eyes, sickened by the lucid recollection of his deep threatening voice. 'He said I knew I wanted it. I didn't. I said no. I tried to go back the way I came but he uh, he grabbed my hair and pulled me into this, um bedroom. He pushed me onto the bed. I was scrambling to get up. He just kept coming on to me. He was pulling up my dress. He kept touching me. I kept pushing him off. I was so scared, I didn't know what to do.

'That's when the other guy came in and pulled him off. They were fighting. The other guy was trying to stop him. They were near the door, so I couldn't get out, but I went over to the corner...uh, there was, uh near a desk. I just wanted to get away from him. I didn't know what was gonna happen. My phone was in the car with my bag, so I couldn't call for help.

'Then the doctor got a uhm hammer from the drawers. I don't know who even keeps a hammer in the drawer, but that is where he got one, I swear! It's like he had planned to attack someone, or maybe for my resistance. I don't know. I thought he was gonna hit me. I thought I was gonna die but then he hit his friend with it... and just kept on striking. With the sharp end, with the two bits. It was loud. It was so loud. That sound. At one point he got it stuck in there, in his stomach and he pushed that man into the corner near me. He knocked some things over. It was so loud.

'I was panicking so I grabbed some scissors from the desk and made a run for it. I just wanted to get out of there. I thought he was going to kill me. But he was fast. He got to me and pulled me back onto the bed again. I kept trying to get away, but I couldn't. He tried to get the scissors from me. Uh then he knocked me down onto the bed, it really hurt. I remember it really hurting. I was crying, I screamed for help. I kept screaming for help. He was climbing on top of me and then he swung his hand, I felt a sharp pain on my head and I blacked out... Next thing I remember is hearing all the noise in here, but I couldn't move, I couldn't see, I couldn't speak...'

Anna took a long deep breath. She'd spoken so frantically trying to get it all out and over with fast, so she could be free of having to recall it. 'That's it, that's what I remember. I don't even know how I got the scissors in my hip, I don't remember that, but that's what they did the surgery for...' she trailed off in a confused state, desperately trying to recall a memory that wasn't there.

Lowe stopped the questioning for a moment. She should have felt a small sense of satisfaction that her assumptions were mostly correct, but she couldn't. All she could see was the woman in front of her, yearning to free her mind of the images, the feelings, the traumas that were now scorched into her brain.

Lowe took a deep breath too. "There in the capacity of Ed Braithwaite's death" she tried to remind herself. They now had an eyewitness who placed the murder weapon in Warren's hands. That was enough to bring him in for questioning at the very least. That would be enough for now. She'd put Anna through more than enough for one day.

'Thank you, Anna. I know how hard that must have been. I think we'll leave it there for now. I just need to ask you to do one more thing and then we'll give you some rest for today. Is that OK?' Lowe got up and walked over to Anna's bedside.

'OK,' Anna wiped her dripping nose. Lowe pulled the table across in front of Anna and placed an image upon it. The photo of Joseph Warren.

'Can you confirm that this is the man who you were with in the house?' Lowe waited for an answer. Anna momentarily froze upon seeing the picture.

Slowly, she nodded.

'I'm sorry Miss Miller, I need you to say it… for the tape.'

'Yes.'

'And how certain would you say you are that the man in this photo, Doctor Joseph Warren, was the man that assaulted you that night?'

Anna's eyes met Lowe's firmly.

'Completely.'

The Funeral

Across town, the heroized celebrity, Doctor J. Warren was tightening the knot of his black tie, completing his black suit. He and his family would soon be heading out to attend their dear friend Eddy's funeral. To finish his outfit, Joseph reached for his designer watch and fastened it around his wrist as Elizabeth emerged from their en-suite bathroom, fitting a black court heel on her right foot. She was dressed in a formal black dress, cut to the knee. They met their similarly dressed teenagers in the hallway, ready to leave. They were, in every way, the perfect reflection of a middle-class family in mourning, and in front of the public, that was the part they would all play.

At the cemetery, where neatly aligned slabs of purposely cut and polished rock protruded repetitively in glum eerie silence, a congregation of black formed a horseshoe around a deep hole in the ground. This was on the nineteenth row of the ninth section in the first plot.

Sombre sunken faces of friends, colleagues and distant relatives of the departed watched as the coffin was lowered slowly and safely into the ground, listening as the vicar offered hopeful prayers for the afterlife and positive messages of remembrance.

Despite the respectable turnout, it was likely that many would forget his death. As a parentless only child, Ed Braithwaite had little family and even littler that he had regularly stayed in touch with. Those that attended the funeral did so purely out of respect, and perhaps a little out of intrigue to meet his famous friend, Doctor J. Warren. The few friends and colleagues Ed had, had made the effort to make an appearance but his passing, his horrifically brutal death, would have little to no significance on their greater lives.

In many ways, it was just like every other funeral. Except for one thing alone: the swarm of story-hungry press junkies waiting for their next fix. The reporters were, however, under strict orders to keep their distance out of respect. Instead, they'd conveniently set up on the path to the exit, ready to intercept the still recovering and grieving doctor.

As the ever-dutiful friend, Joseph stepped forward to say a few words in honour of his close friend and colleague. He took a deep breath and addressed the small crowd, as if making a public speech to hundreds.

'A thanks to those who have come to lay our dear friend, part of our family, to rest. It is with great sadness that this day has arrived so prematurely. Whilst we intend to assure that the woman who caused the death of our Eddy – and almost my own – is convicted and justice is served, today is not about remembering the truly terrible way in which we lost him. Today is about remembering the man and he was a good man.

'Eddy and I met at University, where we became friends for life. He was there through all of the highlights of my life including the birth of my daughter, and later my son. He was best man at my wedding to my dear wife Elizabeth. He was not only a friend, but a trusted colleague. Our only squabble was perhaps over who knew more about the human heart. I'm sure Eddy would laugh knowing I can now say, without argument, that it's me …'

Joseph looked to his wife as he scanned the crowd during his fond words. She was looking into the hole, eyes dry, face motionless. A stark contrast to his children. Grace was crying into her younger brother's shoulder, in similar fashion to other acquaintances. Joseph knew Eddy and Elizabeth had been close, so he'd expected her to be more touched by his words. Yet, she appeared to not be listening. Instead she was still and staring in fixated anger.

Throughout their marriage she'd always remained somewhat of a closed off enigma to him, although he could at the very least deduce typical emotions. Like her, he was angry too in a way. He was angry that the police seemed to be unmoving in their actions when it came to the woman he'd told them had killed Eddy. Perhaps she was still in her coma. Either way, if they were doing their jobs correctly, then the moment she woke up she'd be arrested and charged.

He continued his speech, 'It is with a heavy heart that we say goodbye to our dear Eddy today. A goodbye I didn't plan on saying for a long time yet, but now the time has come. Our memories will always remain with fondness: of your friendship, your intelligence, your generosity, your kindness and your terrible sense of humour.' With his closing line, Joseph turned to the vicar and took a handful of fresh dirt from a dish he was holding. He scattered the dirt into the grave, triggering a chain reaction from the congregation who followed suit.

With that, the funeral came to a close and the party began to disperse down the exit path. Many passed each other, sending reciprocated apologies for the loss, though they would likely all meet again at a pub not far from the cemetery, where a function room was booked for the wake, to toast to Eddy's life and enjoy a warm meal after standing in the cold. A routine send-off, as it were.

The Warren family too, with notable distance between husband and wife, began the short walk down the path, but as the swarm had planned, they were blocked and interrupted by a chorus of questions.

'Doctor Warren how are you feeling about the loss of your friend?'

'Doctor Warren, do you have time for a few questions?'

'Mrs Warren are you glad your husband is OK?'

'Doctor Warren has any action been taken against Miss Miller?'

'Doctor Warren do you think the police are doing their job? Why has no action been taken?'

'Doctor Warren has Anna Miller come out of her coma yet? If so, when will the arrest be made?'

'Doctor Warren do you have anything to say to the public about Ed Braithwaite's death?'

'Doctor Warren...'

'Doctor Warren...'

'Doctor Warren...'

Inundated with the questions and blocked by the press rushing forward and shoving microphones and cameras in their faces, Joseph stopped in his stride, reluctantly causing his family to do so as well. Other attendees looked back on the scene in disgust. Joseph stuck his hands up, ushering them to take a step back.

'Thank you, as you can see, we're currently laying our good friend to rest, please, I plead with you all to have some respect.'

'Doctor Warren what's taking the police so long?'

'Doctor Warren do you know if Miss Miller will be arrested when she wakes up?'

Questions were repeated with absolute disregard for the surroundings and circumstance. Whilst many practiced focuses of media attention could simply say 'no comment' and move on, something within Joseph made him unable to. Perhaps a dire need for attention or even an ulterior motive to control the narrative of his case in the media. However, he was still wary of his family beside him, so he kept it short.

'I'm sure the police are doing everything they can to bring justice for myself and Eddy. I have nothing more to say about Miss Miller. I wish to forget her and move on. Thank you,' he nodded with a closed-mouth smile and turned to leave.

That was until a glaring, unexpected question from a young female journalist, with a short, blonde bob, sent a twang of panic rushing through him.

'Joseph Warren, do you have any comment regarding the rumours of sexual assault?'

'Excuse me?' he turned slowly on the spot.

'There are rumours that you sexually assaulted Anna Miller and that you caused the death of Ed Braithwaite...' As she divulged the speculations, everything went silent. A silence that was only echoed by the sinister location in which the question had been asked. She had picked her timing. Joseph looked directly at the journalist, who had a certain familiarity, yet he could not place her.

'What rumours Dad?' Grace's baby blue eyes widened, horrified and begging for an abrupt denial. The journalist, Elle Mason, stepped back slightly, having been unaware that the doctor's young daughter had been so close before.

Joseph turned to Grace and rubbed her back, 'It's nothing love, just someone trying to make money.'

'So... they're false?' another reporter interjected.

'What?' he spat back, annoyed.

'The rumours that say you sexually assaulted Anna Miller, are they false?' the ignorant journalist tried again. It was a good story. They weren't going to miss it. They didn't care that his family were stood just feet away. They weren't accountable for his actions.

Joseph looked to his wife for support. With a deep betraying glare, Elizabeth turned away from him and began to walk off.

'No!' he shot back to the press vehemently. 'They're not true. I will make no further comment at this time. Thank you,' he turned away and ushered Grace through the crowd and away down the path. Theo followed them, watching his lying father with pure rage.

***

'How did this get out?!' Joseph demanded of his agent down the phone.

'Well I've only just got onto it, but from what I've managed to find out, a couple of papers received an anonymous tip. We're guessing someone who works at the hospital or if it's the press, I guess one of Miller's colleagues. Police can't leak it–'

'I want you to release a statement denying and resenting all accusations. I want it sent to all media outlets immediately!' Joseph yelled into his mobile. 'You better fucking deal with this now. This is my life they're messing with. I didn't do anything. My image will be ruined forever, and my work. You better find out who fucking did this!' Before the agent could reply, Elizabeth knocked on the door of the small cupboard.

'What?!' he screamed through the door.

'People are expecting you in the function room...' she spoke softly. The door flew open abruptly, causing her to take a step back.

'I have more important things to deal with right now!' he huffed.

'There's a time and a place Joe,' she narrowed her eyes at him firmly and unblinking. He snorted a breath and marched past her to continue his performance as the loving, grieving friend, leaving Elizabeth stressed and massaging her forehead with her hand.

Theo walked through to his mother. Ever since the detectives had shown up on their doorstep that day, he'd watched over his mother. He felt instinctively protective. He'd even taken time out from school to ensure she wasn't left alone with their father – not that they were worried given the circumstances and his upstanding grades. He'd barely spoken a word to his father. Not that Joseph had noticed. He seemed blissfully ignorant to the new information his son had acquired about his character.

'You alright Mum?' Theo asked.

Elizabeth lifted her head and forced a smile for her son, 'I'm fine. Let's go in.'

Though unconvinced, he knew now wasn't the time. It was Uncle Eddy's funeral and emotions were running high for everyone. Elizabeth followed her husband into the function room. It was a typical bland room in a typical bland pub. Wooden tables and chairs were set up around the room, with a buffet table of unappealing microwaved or cold food in the corner. The family, friends and colleagues had positioned themselves in small groups around the room.

For the rest of the event, Elizabeth would play the loving mother and housewife again, which came naturally to her. It was a role she'd perfected over the last twenty years. However, now, any time her husband tried to touch her, whether it was a hand on her back or arm or even an accidental graze, she couldn't help but flinch. Something Joseph soon noticed. The drama queen acting up, just when he needed it the least, he thought to himself.

In a small, sparsely occupied corner of the room Grace and Theo were tucking into their selected plates from the buffet.

'Can you believe the press?' Grace somehow managed to shriek in a hushed tone. Theo shrugged, biting into a sandwich from his plate, so she rambled on: 'People sell such lies just to get money with absolutely no consideration of how it can impact the people they're telling lies about. It's sick. Really, disgusting.'

Theo swallowed his bite and turned to his sister, trying very hard not to be astonished by her stupidity at four years his senior.

'How do you know they are lies?' he asked blankly.

Grace screwed up her face. 'What – why would you even ask that?'

'Because Grace, how do you know?'

'I know because Dad says that woman came onto him. He and Uncle Eddy were trying to do something nice and make sure she got home safe. She was a bloody psychopath. Like seriously, who comes into someone's home and attacks one man and kills another with a hammer? If that woman walks free, imagine she can ruin other people's lives like she has ruined ours. I bet she's like woken up and leaked the story. They should lock her up and throw away the key.'

Theo stared at Grace with amazing disbelief. He would have been angry with her, if it weren't for the fact that he would be feeling exactly the same, had he not of overhead the conversation between his mother and Detective Lowe. Her naivety was not her fault. She had been mollycoddled her whole life. She was given everything she ever wanted. She truly believed her dad was a good man and that he was the innocent party.

'Grace, you should just shut up about it. You don't know what you're talking about,' was all Theo could manage.

'Jeez, you sound like Mum. She's been a complete cow to Dad with all this. It's stupid. He needs us. He is trying to play it strong for us you know…what's your problem?'

'You just, you don't know!' Theo snapped at her uncharacteristically, slamming his sandwich down onto the plate.

'I don't know what Theo?'

'…you don't know what happened in that room!'

'Well, neither do you…' she looked to him. The long pause Theo took before responding was enough for Grace to realise his frustration wasn't random. He knew something that she didn't, and immediately she was scared to know what.

'No, but I know someone who does,' he revealed finally. Grace's big blue eyes widened with horror.

'Who?' she tested the shaky question; not sure she was ready to know the answer.

Theo met her eyes and directed her across the room. Grace's world began to alter around her. Her understanding, everything she thought she knew, fell away as the harshness of reality hit her harder than a train. Finally, her gaze met her brother's and landed on its target. Their mother.

Grace gasped as everything began to align.

The Doctor

The day overall had been turbulent for the Warren family and the ride home from the funeral was a silent one. Neither the husband spoke to the wife, nor the wife to the husband, nor the brother to the sister or the sister to the brother. The children evaded the parents and the parents evaded the children. Each remained attuned only to their own internal struggles. A family on the surface with nothing but broken bonds remaining tied only by law or by blood now.

When they got in, both children disappeared quickly to their rooms, needing time alone, Grace especially. Joseph however, was not done. He was angry. His world as he knew it, his reputation, his family, his marriage was crumbling around him. Most importantly, he was losing control of the situation. People were making such horrible accusations. He simply couldn't have that. It was wrong, and it was at the wrong time. How had these rumours gotten out? Who was responsible for it? They would have to pay for what they did. And as for his wife's behaviour over the last few weeks…

'I'm going to bed,' Elizabeth announced coldly, wanting nothing but to shut out the world around her. She was exhausted. Defeated. She went towards the stairs. Joseph scoffed out a sick laugh at her.

She stopped and closed her eyes for one heavy blink, willing Joseph's confrontational manner to dissolve.

'The rumours aren't true Elizabeth. You're acting like a child.'

She said nothing, passive as ever, which only served to further provoke him. He wanted, nay, craved the reaction. He needed to have a fight that he would win. He had to regain some control over something and he knew she would be the easiest target. She always had been.

He walked over to her, his tall, ominous frame shadowing her, and those icy blue eyes slicing into her own.

'Did you hear me?'

'Yes.'

'Then why? Why are you acting like that, hmm?'

'Like what?'

'Moving away every time I touch you. What's that about? Is it cause some woman made false accusations to the press. You know that's a risk, there's always a risk with the media that someone will sell lies for money. You know that.' He put his hands on either side of her shoulders and sunk down to her level to meet her, imposing eye to fearful eye. Elizabeth did not move, scared that if she did, she would further arouse him. Joseph released another laugh.

'Look at you. I'm still me. I'm still your husband. There's nothing to be afraid of…'

'Are they true?' she waited, giving him a chance to be honest with her. He released her, his arms flopping to his sides. She had aggravated him. He inhaled, stroking his chin in one tight motion.

'You're being very silly now Elizabeth,' his lips narrowed enunciating each word, his tone becoming more threatening. She knew all too well where this would end.

'I'm going to bed,' she repeated adamantly, turning once more.

Joseph grabbed her arm firmly, pulling her back. He twisted her so that she had no choice but to look at him. Then he pushed her up against the wall, his palm clasping at her neck tightly. He positioned his face as close to hers as he could get, their noses practically touching. Through nasty gritted teeth, that sprayed spit into her face at each plosive sound, Joseph began to tell her exactly what she would do.

'No Elizabeth dearest. You will stop this. You will stop this n–'

A hard knock at the door.

Joseph's head shot towards it. They weren't expecting company. He looked to it for a moment but remained gripping Elizabeth's neck so tightly that white halos formed on her skin around his fingertips. She tried to look at the door, praying for him to open it and let her go.

The visitors knocked again. Joseph's focus spun back to his wife. He put an unwavering finger to his lips.

Another knock. This time, it attracted the attention of Theo, who left his room to see why his parents weren't answering the door, Grace following closely behind him. They would not make it down in time to witness their father's hands around their mother's neck. Joseph always knew when to let go. He exhaled angrily and released Elizabeth. Free of him, she stroked her own neck soothingly.

'Doctor Warren? Doctor Warren!' Another more rapid knock with a call through. Whoever it was, was not going to go away. Joseph yanked open the door.

'Yes?!' he regretted saying instantly when he saw the two uniformed police officers standing on his doorstep, flashing blue lights drawing attention behind them.

'You're Joseph Warren?' one of them asked.

'I am. What's–'

'Sir, we need you to come with us to the station for questioning, now please.'

'Dad...?' Grace called uncertainly. Joseph looked back to see the lasting image of his family standing in the hallway, his wife a portrait of fear, his son a statue of anger and the apple of his eye like a puppy in a storm.

'Oh, this is ridiculous!' he flapped his arms about. Could his day get any worse? Why was everyone being so difficult? He hadn't done anything wrong, he was an upstanding member of the community, one of the most talented and intelligent cardiologists in the country and a fantastic husband and father – or so his inflated ego would have him delude himself.

'Doctor Warren, I'm sorry but I need you to come with us now please.' The officer was not to be argued with and Joseph couldn't take the risk that the paparazzi could be lurking after the rumours that were circulated earlier in the day. Resisting would only damage his image.

'Fine. Fine,' he stepped outside with the officers and was shown into the back of the police car.

'Mrs Warren,' the other officer called into the house, unaware that their timing had saved Elizabeth from the frightening encounter that had occurred just moments before between man and wife. 'You may want to phone your husband's lawyer.'

The Interrogation

Bricks were painted with a faint grey. The tiny square windows near the ceiling streamed small bursts of fading daylight down onto the old, scratched table. To complete the dark, dingy interrogation room: four chairs, fluorescent strip lights and a one-way mirror on the wall next to the door. Inside, Joseph was sat in the far chair, leaning back with one arm rested on the table. He drummed his fingers repetitively. He was waiting.

Behind the one-way glass, Lowe and Hayes stood watching him. What they needed more than anything was a confession. They were still waiting on the DNA evidence to place the murder weapon in his hands for certain. At this stage, it was unlikely that they could charge him based solely on Anna Miller's account. All they needed was for him to make one slip up, just one mistake. It wouldn't be easy. He was a smart man. He'd managed to use his position to manipulate and control the narrative surrounding the case to the wider world through the media. He'd managed to make an old charge against him evaporate. He'd managed to recount a credible version of events.

No matter the difficulty, Lowe knew she had to try. For Ed, who had lost his life, and for Anna, who, although physically alive, would be mentally scarred for the rest of hers.

'Let's go and break this son of a bitch,' Lowe marched into the interview room, Hayes following behind her.

'Hello again Doctor Warren, thank you for coming in,' Hayes began as they both took their seats opposite Joseph.

'I don't believe you left me much choice,' he sneered.

Hayes chose to ignore Joseph's tone and continued pleasantly, 'Can we get you anything before we start?'

'Yes, how about my lawyer?'

'Interesting. It's only the guilty ones that ask for the lawyer first,' Lowe leaned in. Joseph mimicked her body language, placing both elbows on the table and clasping his hands together, putting his head up on them. He smiled deprecatingly, eyeing up Lowe.

'Quite a determined one aren't you, Detective?' he mocked. He knew he could get under her skin if he pushed hard enough and he might just have some fun doing it. She wasn't as tough as she made out; no one ever was.

Lowe did not retaliate to his words.

'So, why am I here? No! Don't tell me. Let me guess,' Joseph leaned back again. 'Little Miss Murderer woke up from her coma and passed her guilt onto me?' he cocked a conceited eyebrow.

The detectives waited for him to get his arrogant, self-indulgent speech out of the way. It wasn't uncommon in criminals who believed they were smarter and above the law, so they let him continue, watching him amused. This sad pathetic excuse for a man, expecting he would walk away unscathed and unpunished.

'Hmm, pin the blame on the man who survived her attack, very clever of her. Now I can understand *her* taking sides,' Joseph pointed disgustedly to Lowe. 'You know, women helping women, in this new societal defiance against the patriarchy. But you...' he tilted his head towards Hayes, '...you believed her too. An educated man such as yourself. Hah! Miss Miller must be a very good storyteller, but then, I guess that is her job.

'So, you see, the fact of the matter is, I'm not requesting my lawyer because I'm guilty, no. I'm requesting him because you two are noticeably biased detectives, who believed a woman who cried wolf and have decided to pull me in for questioning purely based on someone's lies – without any evidence. Therefore, I think I'm within my rights here... no?' He looked between them expectantly.

'Why do you assume we've pulled you in for questioning because of Anna Miller?' Lowe tilted her head to the side, mocking his own body language but also curious to see his reaction. Joseph's face dropped, his eyes narrowing at her as he prepared his response. Before he could explain himself, Lowe spoke to her partner.

'DI Hayes, could you see to it that Mr Warren's lawyer is brought in please?'

'Sure thing,' Hayes got up and left the room. Lowe looked to Joseph and smiled, ready.

'So, Mr Warren, would you like to know why you are here, while we wait?'

'My title is Doctor, Detective,' he corrected her sourly.

Lowe smirked. She knew this. She was intentionally addressing him incorrectly to ruffle his feathers. She knew his status meant everything to him and that being degraded by a woman, of all people, would really hurt his ego.

'You're proud of your career, Mr Warren?' she bided her time, waiting for Hayes to return. Joseph crossed his arms.

'I've helped save hundreds of lives. Wouldn't you be?' he boasted. Lowe stuck out her bottom lip and nodded.

'Actually, whilst we're waiting, d'you mind if I ask you a medical question? Friend of mine, she's a cyclist, had an accident the other day.'

'Go ahead,' Joseph agreed carefully, trying not to let his confusion show. What was she up to?

'These bones here, these ribs...' Lowe pushed back her jacket, becoming consciously aware that her shirt was tighter than she'd thought, which coincidentally may help her unsettle Joseph. On her own body, she indicated to the same ribs that had been broken and splintered on Ed Braithwaite, '...are they easier to break than the top ones?'

'That would depend entirely on how they were broken,' Joseph said simply, brushing her off, without even looking.

He wasn't going to play Lowe's game. If she'd have been a blonde, maybe he'd have been unable to resist granting himself a look, but he had to be on his best behaviour in here. He couldn't let this detective who had it in for him know any wiser. Though, she would have been an easy target, he thought to himself. She was clearly lonely. Obviously constantly and obsessively distracted by a case. There would be ample opportunity. It would be so easy to take her down.

'OK, but let's say these ones were broken, would it cause more internal damage, is there a greater risk of say... puncturing a lung with these lower ones compared to the upper ones?'

'My specialism is the heart...I really couldn't say.'

'Really?' Lowe leaned forward in taunting disbelief. 'With all those years of medical training, you can't answer a simple medical question? I have to say Doctor, I'm disappointed,' Lowe was playing it cool but annoyingly, he wasn't giving her anything.

'Well now Detective, with all this training you must have had to make Chief Inspector no doubt... surely you can do better than that?' A crooked smirk brushed across his lips and his piercing blue eyes gleamed with pleasure. Lowe sat back, the deep sense of loathing she felt for Joseph making his physical closeness repulsive to her.

Outside the room, the lawyer had been ready and waiting all along and Hayes had been watching Joseph's interactions with Lowe outside. He knew in that moment, and with absolute conviction, that she had been right all along. This man had committed the crimes on the case they were investigating. What's more, he fully intended to get away with it.

Hayes called in the lawyer and re-entered.

'Joe,' the lawyer shook his client's hand and placed a black briefcase on the table. From it, he took out his own Dictaphone and pressed record. 'Have they forced you to say anything without a lawyer present yet?' he signalled scornfully to the detectives as he asked the question.

'Not at all. The Detective Chief Inspector and I were just having a lovely chat about her friend's cycling accident,' Joseph smiled wryly.

'Right... well, is my client under arrest?'

'No. He is a suspect in our investigation into the death of Edward Braithwaite,' Lowe explained simply to the lawyer. He was just another suited city man, caring more about his profit than his morals.

'Right, well Detective, I think it would be best if we get to the questions, as you know, you can't hold my client for too long if you aren't going to arrest or charge him.' The lawyer sat. 'When you're ready...'

'Uh, right, OK, let's start with what happened on the night of Ed Braithwaite's death, shall we. If you can just tell us again what you think happened on that night,' Hayes began.

'What I know happened that night, was that Eddy and I met and went for drinks at Zero. In the bar we met a group of girls. As I told you before, I don't remember all their names, but this woman, Anna Miller, was one of them, obviously. When we went to leave, around half ten, we offered her a lift home. We didn't want her to get a taxi because the station was on our way and it costs a lot. This is the capital after all. We saw no danger in it.'

'To confirm, after consuming alcohol, you allowed your friend Ed Braithwaite to drive yourself and another?' Lowe interjected.

'Yes. That was a mistake. I will admit that.' Joseph looked to his lawyer for assurance. The lawyer nodded so he continued, 'She got in, Eddy dropped me off first as it was closest. When we got to mine, she said she needed to use the toilet and was desperate. Seeing no problem with this, I let her in to use the bathroom on that level. Instead, she simply threw herself at me, sexually speaking. I mean, I understand the effect I can have on women, but I'm a happily married man, so I tried to get her off.

'She got angry and started throwing things, she broke one of the glass tumblers I'd left on the desk. She grabbed scissors and started attacking me. Luckily, Eddy came in and tried to help, but she went full on at him with the scissors. It was crazy. I rushed to grab anything to help defend myself. I picked up a hammer, it was the first thing I could get my hands on and went back in. There was a scuffle. Scissors and hammer had changed all around. She struck Eddy and he'd fallen over in the corner, she kept striking him, so I pulled her back, we fell onto the bed. Then she stabbed me with the scissors and everything blacked out.'

His recount was similar to his original. Clear. Linear. Rehearsed. The glaring difference – and what would prove a problem for the detectives – was that originally, he'd placed the murder weapon in his own hands. In this one, he'd left it vague. Lowe pulled out a photo taken from the post-mortem and threw it down in front of Joseph.

'The wounds that killed your friend, they're there in that picture, can you tell me how he sustained these injuries?'

Joseph pretended to be shocked by the photos and looked away. His disgruntled lawyer handed them back to Lowe.

'Can you tell me how Ed Braithwaite came to suffer those fatal wounds?' she repeated.

'Yes. As I said, Anna Miller attacked him.'

'Anna Miller attacked him?'

'Yes.'

'Anna Miller who had the scissors?'

'Yes.' Joseph was growing agitated.

'Anna Miller, an average sized woman, somehow managed to stab your fairly large friend Ed Braithwaite four times in the side without much resistance, breaking multiple ribs, causing a lot of internal damage and puncturing his lung with just a pair of household scissors?'

'You don't have to answer that,' the lawyer interjected, but Joseph already knew how to answer.

'No Detective. That's not what I said. You first asked if Anna Miller attacked him. She did. You then asked if she'd had the scissors. She had. You inferred that I said she attacked him with the scissors. I did not. Clearly, she hit him with the hammer,' Joseph spoke calmly.

'Clearly?'

'Clearly.'

'So how did she come to get the hammer? You said you went and got it,' Hayes, finally chipping in, waited for more information.

'I told you, there was a scuffle. I guess whilst I was trying to prevent damage from the scissors, she managed to grab the hammer.' He wasn't giving them anything. He was too clever and with his lawyer present, there was little more they could do to push him. He was on his best behaviour.

'I'd like to ask on what grounds it is that you place my client as a suspect? I'm not hearing any. If anything, it seems we should be looking to press charges.' The lawyer was growing impatient.

'The issue is, in Joseph's own original statement he told us that he was holding the hammer, which would be consistent with the injuries and therefore place him as Ed Braithwaite's killer...' Hayes elaborated, giving up their only leverage.

'With all due respect Detective, you visited me a day after surgery, whilst I was on some very strong painkillers, so you can hardly punish me for misplacing a few details here and there. I can share with you the effects of pain medication and trauma, if this would be useful for your investigation?' He was patronising them in a tone only detectable to them. To an outsider, it would appear that Joseph was just trying to be helpful and open about his willingness to help in their investigation.

'So, you have no actual evidence or anything indicating my client is responsible for the death of Ed Braithwaite?' the lawyer asked again, more forcibly. The detectives were left speechless.

'Oh dear, looks like your time's up, Detective,' Joseph said smugly. He'd won this round and he knew it.

Lowe closed her eyes. Anything else was pointless now. They had nothing but a man's word against a woman's, each blaming the other. She knew very well which of them the system would believe. This interrogation was over. She had failed.

The *Detective*

'Lowe!' Tabbot bellowed into the bullpen of detectives, officers and administrators. It had been a long and exhausting day and all Lowe wanted right now was to go home and shut the world away.

Those working in the room stopped their activities and looked to her. A worried expression jumped into Haye's features. Lowe hadn't even had a chance to sit down since returning from Warren's questioning and the last thing she needed right now was to be shouted at and scolded by Tabbot. Then again, she also expected it. She had messed up. Big time.

'Lowe! Get in here now!' Tabbot screeched. She sighed and went into his office, closing the door behind her. She stood opposite him, arms crossed, waiting. She didn't care what he had to say. None of that mattered now. She had failed Anna. She'd let the case get the better of her and had made too many mistakes. She was done here. She knew it. She'd be off the case and Joseph Warren would walk free.

'What the fuck were you thinking Abigail?! Showing up with flashing blue lights and uniforms at his house. Bringing him in and for what Abbie? For what?! Nothing!'

'Sir, I–'

'Look, look! Just look at what you've done!' He scrambled for the remote to switch on a small TV mounted on the wall in his office. His hands were shaking so much from anger that it took him a moment to turn the thing on.

Lowe looked. A news reel, a reporter midframe, then the images of Joseph being taken away in the police car she'd sent, a scrolling banner, questioning headline. The media.

'Why would you allow this circus to happen? What were you thinking, taking an innocent public figure in a police car without any evidence? How many times Detective? How many times do I have to tell you? You need hard fucking evidence! You can't keep harassing Joe. I'm in half a mind to take you off the case.'

'I thought we had enough to question him. An eyewitness who says he murdered his friend and attacked her. That's pretty compelling.'

'He too, claimed to be an eyewitness to a murder and to being attacked. Did you interrogate Miss Miller in the same respect?' he raised his eyebrows angrily. She said nothing but looked down to the floor.

'Well, did you?' he asked again impatiently.

'No,' she replied loudly. Tabbot flopped down into his chair and heaved out a sigh, shaking his head.

'Go home Lowe,' he dismissed her. He was so angry he couldn't even look at her, but was sure to add, 'And whatever's distracting you from investigating this case properly – fix it, before you make another mistake. Next time, it'll be your badge.'

Lowe left swiftly and upset. She was still on the case, but for what? She was exhausted. She was responsible. She was angry. She picked up her bag and rushed out, ignoring Hayes as he called after her to ask if she was OK.

How had she let everything get away from her? She was sure she knew what she was doing, but she'd let her impulses get the better of her. She'd acted purely on whims over facts. That wasn't like her at all, and it was going to cost her. She was both lucky and grateful that Tabbot hadn't taken her off the case. If she was in his position, she would have done. She was on extremely thin ice now, one more mistake and she would lose her job, but if she lost it, she had nothing. No one. Her job was everything. Why couldn't she just let her bias go? What the fuck was her problem?

She didn't know what to do. She didn't even know where she was going really, she just drove. Without thinking, she was driving to the place she always went to feel better, to feel safe.

She pulled up and parked outside Rob's apartment block.

As she suddenly realised where she was, Lowe rested her head on the wheel, breathing. Just breathing. What was she doing? She shouldn't be here. He had told her it was over. He couldn't do it anymore. What was she thinking? She looked up and over to the floor of his apartment. She didn't care. After everything that had happened, she needed him tonight.

She pulled the key out of the ignition. Just one last time.

Lowe got out of the car, slamming the door behind her and walked into the block. In the lobby, she pressed the button for the lift. It was in use. Impatient, she went for the stairs and raced up them with purpose to his floor. She went through the double doors to the balcony, ready to knock on his door.

The elevator dinged and opened. Lowe retreated, hiding herself behind a bend. Rob exited the lift with another person. A woman.

Lowe watched from her position, frozen. He was smiling, happy. The mystery woman was too, and she was attractive. Dressed up. Rob put his hand on her back, unlocked his door and they went in, unaware of their spectator. The door closed behind them.

Lowe released the breath she'd been holding in and stared for a long while. What had she done? She turned, defeated and walked back down the stairs to her car. She banged her head on the wheel, frustrated with herself before putting the keys in the ignition, her foot on the clutch and driving off.

On her way home, she pulled up outside a late-night pharmacy on the high street and went in. She picked out two items and went to the counter. One a long blue rectangle box. The other a sickly pink bottle. She needed to get rid of the sickening feeling in her stomach. She gave the cashier a quick smile as the items were processed.

'Will that be all?' the cashier asked in that almost automated customer service voice.

'Uh, yeah. Thanks,' Lowe said, looking around her, wishing the cashier would hurry.

'Alright then, that'll be fifteen pounds twenty-eight please,' the cashier forced a smile, waiting for payment. Lowe fumbled around in her pockets, pulling out her card to pay. Upon receipt, she went to grab her purchases.

'Oh Miss, if that comes back positive…' the cashier pointed to the box, '…then don't take that.' She then indicated to the bottle of Pepto-Bismol. Lowe took the two items and nodded a thanks before driving the rest of the way home.

***

Lowe's flat was small, simple and practical. It had a distinctly green colouring from the panels throughout and was mostly open plan. It was clean and barely looked lived in, although she had lived there for years. It wasn't that she was a neat freak or anything, it's just that her job had kept her busy and she was seldom home. Similarly, she could definitely afford something nicer or bigger, but this flat had started as somewhere to rest her head twelve years ago and had stuck. She'd rented from the same landlord who never complained and gave her privacy. To her, it was home. The only home she'd ever really known.

She threw her jacket down on the sofa and placed her pharmacy things on the kitchen counter, staring between them, her arms outstretched either side as she deliberated. This was the last thing she needed. She'd been putting it off for so long, scared of the outcome. She closed her eyes, took a deep breath and grabbed the box, heading into the bathroom.

Minutes later, she reappeared with the white stick and paced the room, tapping it against one of her hands as she waited. Nothing.

Another pace. Nothing.

Another pace. Nothing.

She dropped down onto the sofa, stick still in hand. Why did it take so long? She placed her elbow on her knee and rested her head in her hand, blowing out air as she waited. Finally, the test result faded into the small circular window. She looked at it, eyes widening. She gave it a shake just to be sure, but the result remained. It was now permanent.

Lowe's hands fell between her legs as she looked around her empty, lonely apartment. She looked at the shelves that should have been filled but displayed only a few work-related books. She looked at the kitchen, where an empty fridge stood atop an empty freezer. Over in the bedroom, a double bed for one. In front of her, a coffee table with coasters still in a stack because they'd never been used. This couldn't happen. Everything was going wrong.

'Fuck,' she exhaled, lifting the test to check it once again, as if it would change. 'Fuck,' she repeated louder, the reality of her situation settling in. Her breath began to get heavy. 'Fuck. Fuck.

Fuck. Fuck. FUUUUUUUUCCCCCKKK!' she shouted, hurling the test across the room.

It hit the wall with an echoing bang and fell to the floor.

The Confrontation

As Lowe's life began to fall apart that night, Elizabeth was about to change hers. Her husband's actions were now affecting her children and she couldn't let that happen. She had to find the strength to stand up to him. It was overdue. Long overdue.

In anticipation of Joseph's return, she had sent the kids to their grandparents. Initially, Grace protested, but Theo had managed to persuade her it was best for them to go. As much as he didn't want to leave his mother alone with their father when he returned, he knew this was something she needed to do by herself.

Elizabeth knew he'd be coming home. She knew more than anyone just how clever and manipulating her husband could be. She knew it wouldn't take long for him to worm his way out of questioning and back into his beloved house. When he arrived, she would be waiting, and she would be ready.

The keys jangled in the keyhole and the lock turned. Joseph was home. He'd walked free. It was a close call, but he'd managed to wiggle himself out of it. There wasn't any way they'd be able to pin responsibility for Eddy's death on him now. They had nothing. He'd made sure of that. There was only one piece of damning evidence he needed to find and destroy, in case that detective decided to get a warrant to search the house. It had to be there. If the police didn't have it, it had to still be in the house.

For Joseph, the frustrating and somewhat terrifying thing was: it wasn't where he'd hidden it before he'd set about making his actions look like an accident by opening scissors and forcing them into both Anna's body and his own and knocking himself out with some sleeping pills. He'd even thrown and smashed the glass of water he'd used to take the tablets, to add to the scene of a struggle.

He hadn't meant for it to escalate. If it hadn't been for Eddy interrupting, everything would have gone smoothly that night. He hadn't intended to kill Eddy, but Eddy should have known better than to interrupt him when he was having his fun. As for the girl, he hadn't intended to knock her out either. He just wanted to have sex with her, he didn't understand why all her screaming and fighting was necessary. It just made it harder for him to get what he wanted. He had just needed her to be quiet. After all, he didn't want to inconvenience the neighbours. It was all Eddy's fault for interrupting. If he had just stayed in the car long enough for Joseph to have his way, none of this would have happened. Eddy would still be alive, and Joseph would have made sure that weak blonde journalist kept her beautiful little mouth shut.

Eddy had ruined everything, so he'd had to think on his feet. That meant covering up and hiding any evidence that could condemn him, including this one item he was looking for now. As he entered the house, Joseph went directly into the living room, switching on a standing lamp. He scurried through the kitchen and down to the basement. He searched rampantly through the room. It wasn't there. He tried the bathroom and garage on the same level. Both clear.

Growing impatient, he raced back up the stairs to the kitchen. He yanked open drawers, rifling through cutlery and utensils noisily, leaving a mess as he went. He pulled open the cupboards. He looked over the room. Still, there was no trace of what he wanted. Back into the living room. He scanned over every shelf, he lifted off the sofa cushions, pulled out the storage baskets in the unit, throwing out objects that were not the focus of his search.

Stressed and heavy-breathed, Joseph ran his hands through his hair. He was beginning to panic. He looked over to the hallway where he'd entered. Through the open arch he could see the shoebox, fixed to the wall with a mantle over it and littered with dust-collecting ornaments. He hurried to it and began to pull out the rush baskets full of shoes. Suddenly, the dim light in the hallway flicked on. Startled, Joseph halted his hunt.

'Looking for something?' Elizabeth had been sat on the stairs all along. She had listened as he'd rushed around looking for the incredibly important item. Waiting. Waiting for him to notice her. She stood up from the stairs. He watched her. It could just have been the dark portentous shadows produced by the little light available in the hallway, but something seemed different about her. Chilling.

'Elizabeth...' he straightened himself slowly, watching fixedly as she ever so slowly moved her right arm. On the small round table next to the stairs, she placed down the object of his desire.

Joseph's eyes flicked between his wife and the camera.

He lurched forward.

'Ah. Don't,' Elizabeth warned him, holding out a large and freshly sharpened kitchen knife. He stopped in his tracks and held up his hands. Something within him was oddly excited by his wife's apparent moment of triumph. He'd lived with Elizabeth for nearly twenty years, and this was the first time she'd shown any sign of fighting back. Frankly, he was impressed that she'd even found the courage to try this. Pity she'd never see it through. She didn't have it in her.

'Now, Elizabeth...come on. Let's not do anything we might regret.' He edged closer to her, his hands still in the air. She remained standing, the knife outstretched, both hands shaking uncontrollably as she faced the man who had tortured her for so long.

'Don't,' she repeated defiantly.

'I know you don't want to hurt me Elizabeth, come now. Put the knife down.'

As her hands steadied, he stopped his approach. He looked to her and smirked. He was unnerving her.

'Mrs Warren, I'm impressed. How strong you must think you are.'

'Fitting isn't it?' she hissed, a spiteful look on her face. 'Your little housewife armed with nothing but a kitchen knife.'

Joseph let out a shrill laugh. She must have rehearsed that line and had obviously looked forward to saying it.

'You must stop this silliness Wife. It doesn't suit you. Now hand me the knife.' He held out his hand, waiting expectantly. Elizabeth hesitated. He took a deep breath, prepared to break her down even more.

'No,' she said shakily.

'Come on Dear, I know you don't want to hurt me. You love me. I'm your husband. You know we're right for each other. Let's just put the knife down. I'm free now, we can move on from this. We can move on together, be a happy family. We can go on that holiday you've always wanted, with the kids, I'll take time off. Come on, you know it will be fun!'

'No, we can't...' she breathed.

'Yes! Yes, we can. All this will be over. I won't hurt you anymore. I'll keep you safe. I'll give you everything you need. Come on Lizzy. You know I love you. You know you love me. This is all means nothing. You are all that matters.'

Elizabeth swallowed. The knife began to lower at his words.

'That's it, good girl. We can do this. Come here.'

Joseph moved into her body, taunting the fire in front of him, using his power over her once again. Seemingly defeated, Elizabeth allowed him to run his hands around her waist and pull her in. He traced a long finger across her soft cheek. Standing on the tips of her toes, she raised her chin to his ear.

'Oh, Joe,' she whispered. The corner of his mouth twitched. He knew she didn't have it in her. She retreated down to her normal height and was outwardly captivated by the spell of his mesmerising blue eyes.

Her eyes narrowed.

'I'd have used a hammer, but it seems ours is being held as a murder weapon,' Elizabeth smiled maliciously.

His face dropped.

'Why you!' She'd touched his trigger. Losing his temper, Joseph leapt forward in attempt to grab the knife from Elizabeth's hands, but she reacted quickly and slashed him. He groaned in pain and retreated.

'You bitch!' he spat, cradling his wounded hand.

'If you come one step closer, I will do even more damage to your precious appearance.' Elizabeth waited for him to try again, but it appeared he'd received her message loud and clear, so she went on, as he held pressure on his bleeding palm.

'Did you honestly think I wouldn't find it?' Elizabeth motioned to the camera. 'I found the sleeping pills too. Impressive, I'll give you that Joe. How you made it look like you were a victim. Didn't plan on killing Eddy, did you? No. But he got in the way, didn't he? You just meant to knock him out. But you liked it, didn't you? The blood. The power. The control. So, you murdered your best friend.

You went at him, again and again, bludgeoning him with that hammer. It's all right there on the camera–'

'Shut up. Shut up! You shut it now,' Joseph roared at her, but she wasn't done.

'What a bonus, I mean I know you like recording the sex but now you have your little video to marvel in murdering Eddy too. And what about the girl? What was it, you weren't sure how you were going to keep this one quiet? You couldn't marry her... no. Not like you married me, so I'd keep my mouth shut. You must have panicked. You've never gotten away with murder before, and how would you, with a witness? Killing her too and making it look like an accident must have been the only option.

'But she didn't die. You didn't hit her hard enough. You thought you did though, didn't you? That's why you tried to make it look like an accident. You thought you'd be the only one to live to tell the tale and then you'd have won the ultimate prize, getting away with murder. It must be killing you that she's woken up and told the truth. Am I right?' Elizabeth looked to him with an expression full of pure and visceral hatred.

'I don't have to listen to this,' he shook his head and walked through into the living room. Elizabeth followed him, stopping in the centre of the arch that divided the two rooms.

'AM I RIGHT?!' she screamed at him, anger furiously rushing through every vein in her body.

'I gave you a good life woman, I've provided you with everything. You ungrateful cow!' he shouted back.

'A good life? A good life!' Elizabeth released a hysterical cackle. 'I was young. It was my first year on campus. You didn't even give me a chance! You just took me and then when I got pregnant you manipulated me into marrying you. I should never have let you near our daughter.'

'That's a lie! I have given you everything you could ever wish for.'

'Given me everything? Hah. You have some nerve. In taking my body you took my degree, my career, you took away my life as I wanted to live it, and you stored me up in your grand house as nothing more than a trophy!'

'No Elizabeth. No. I've cared for you. I've given you everything you wanted. That girl, she was just a mistake. A slip up. An accident.'

'An accident? You *raped* her. And you recorded it, you sick fuck.'

'You're wrong. She wanted it. She drunk with us, she flirted, she got into our car, she invited herself in. She wanted it. I mean, did you see what she was wearing? That skimpy dress in the middle of winter. She wanted it.'

'No. No Joseph. She didn't. Her screams were screams of pain. Not pleasure. And what she was wearing had nothing to do with it. You can't shoot someone dead and say they wanted it because they weren't wearing a bullet proof vest.' Elizabeth was nauseated, looking at the wretched beast that had manipulated her into marrying him.

How had she allowed herself to be abused by him again and again? If she'd have found the courage to speak up all those years ago, if she'd have just found the strength, none of this would have happened. Eddy would have been alive. She would have been happy. Anna would have been safe. Joseph would have been punished, just as he deserved. She shouldn't have given in to the pressure all those years ago, but no one believed her, and she'd let them convince her that it was her fault. That she had asked for it. That she had been irresponsible. That Joseph had done nothing wrong.

She stood still for a moment, glaring and pointed the knife at him. A long silence ensued between them. A silence that ended their marriage. A silence that ended his hold over her. A silence that freed her.

'What are you going to do?' Joseph asked finally. Elizabeth looked up, her arms falling to her sides.

'I want you to leave. You will file for divorce first thing in the morning. You will leave me the house and full custody of the children. Our lawyers will agree on the financial sum for their support. You will not attempt to contact them. You will not see them. You will not touch them—'

'No. No. Elizabeth please. I love them. I love the kids. You know I love them. You know I'd never hurt them Elizabeth, you can't take my kids away from me, I'd never hurt them.' He moved towards her, ready to beg, but her arm shot up once more with the knife.

'No. You won't. I won't let you. They are my children and you won't go near them again. If you so much as try, I will personally hand that video tape in to the police. Without hesitation. Do you understand?'

'You can't take them. You can't. Please don't do this.' Joseph had lost all control. He was begging now. Pleading with his wife. 'Please, Elizabeth, what kind of mother doesn't let her children see their father?'

'What kind of mother let's her son and her daughter think it is OK to protect a man like you?'

She had rendered him speechless. He stood. Powerlessly, he waited for her to change her mind, but she wasn't the woman he'd once been able to control. He had no power over her now. He was done. He had no choice. He looked to her, trying to catch her eye, but she would not falter. He walked forward, and she moved aside to let him out. He dropped his keys on the mantel and left through the front door of his home for the final time.

As the black door of number twenty-nine closed behind him, Elizabeth rushed forward and locked it, before dropping the knife from her stiffened hand and collapsing into a heap on the floor, tears pouring out. She'd done it. She'd finally gotten rid of him, and of the burden that had tortured her internally for so long. She exhaled a sigh of relief. For the first time in twenty years, she smiled a real smile. With joyous tears trickling down her lifted cheeks, happiness washed over her. He was gone.

She got up, picked up the camera, and freshened herself up. She was going to see her children. When the divorce was settled, she'd sell this house and make a new start for her family. Right now, all she wanted was to be with her children. Once ready, she locked the door and jumped in her car, driving forward to start her promising future.

The Divorce

'Abbie? Abbie!' Hayes called through the door to the flat. 'Abs, I know you're in there, come on, it's me. Open up.'

Hayes had gone over to Lowe's flat to check that she was alright. She'd not shown up for work that morning, which was weird. In all the years he'd worked alongside her, he'd never seen her take a day off and after the interrogation and rollicking from Tabbot yesterday, he was convinced something must be wrong.

'I'm sick,' she shouted loud enough for him to hear through the door. He rested his forehead against it. He wasn't going to give up, so she'd have to open up eventually.

'No, you're not. I know you, c'mon, is this about the case?'

She didn't reply. At that moment a neighbour exited and stared at Hayes. He nodded awkwardly as she studied him suspiciously. He guessed it was probably unusual for Lowe to have visitors, especially so early in the morning.

He waited for the neighbour to disappear before trying again. 'It's not your fault Abbie. Open up. We can still solve this. We can still get him.'

'It's not about the case,' she called. His head retreated from the door revealing his double chin. He wasn't expecting that.

'Then what's it about?' he waited for her to reply. Again, she didn't. He knocked one more time, 'Just open the door Abbie, we can–'

The door flung open.

'–talk,' he finished, looking at his colleague. This was not the Lowe he was used to seeing. Her usual plain pantsuit had been replaced with sweats and an oversized jumper. The usually kempt ponytail was rolled in a greasy, floppy mess on her head. Her eyes were red raw from exhaustion. Hayes had never seen her quite like this.

He stepped inside and closed the door behind him as she returned to lazing in defeat on the sofa. He scanned over her flat. It was exactly the kind of place he imagined Lowe living in. He sat on the coffee table opposite her, moving the stack of coasters out of the way and looked at Lowe compassionately. It was the first time he'd seen her this despairing.

'What am I doing Ellis? How did I let this happen?' her eyes flicked up hopelessly. Hayes believed her questions to be connected to the case.

'These things happen. You know that,' he offered, unsure of how to console his partner.

'I've failed.'

'What did that arsehole Tabbot say?'

Lowe realised then that Hayes' mind was still firmly on the case.

'No. Nothing…' She shook her head and recited the endless thoughts relating to the investigation that had been swirling around her brain. 'It just makes me sick. We know he is guilty, but we can't prove it. He's made sure of that. But that doesn't change the fact that he did it. I feel like the entire system, and yeah Tabbot especially, is just this massive obstacle standing in the way of justice. The victim, she deserves more. She is a human being Ellis and she was hurt... and I, I can't help her. I don't know what to do.'

Hayes watched her sympathetically for a moment, as she wiped her nose on her sleeve, rubbed her eyes and composed herself. He wasn't judging her. He was there to listen and to support her. Not only as her colleague, as her friend. But as her friend and partner at work, he knew he had to get her back on her feet.

'I'll tell you what you're going to do.' Hayes rose from the coffee table. She looked up at him. 'You're going to get up. You're going to get in the bloody shower, cause if I'm honest Abs, you stink, and then you're going to get dressed and you're going to come to the office with me and do whatever it takes to put that sick shit Warren behind bars, cause that's your job. We've got a case to solve. And you won't help Anna Miller by sitting on your arse now, will you?' he raised his eyebrows, pointing to what he presumed was her bathroom, waiting for her to oblige.

She deliberated for a moment.

'Come on. Up you get, no slacking on the job,' he scolded her in a jokey and endearing way. He was right. She couldn't give up now. She had a responsibility to solve this case and she'd promised herself she'd do whatever it takes. Lowe stood up finally, thanks to the much-needed kick from her partner and made her way to the bathroom.

'And Abs?'

'Yeah?'

'Whatever happens, what matters is that you didn't stop trying.'

She nodded a meaningful acknowledgement, grateful for his support. This man was more than a colleague to her. He was like family and pretty soon, she was going to need that support more than ever.

***

After she'd freshened up, Lowe and Hayes began driving back to the office to continue work on the case.

'Still nothing from forensics, checked this morning. It's weird. I'm not sure what's taking the lab so long. Never normally takes this long,' Hayes ranted.

He was right. It was unusual for the results to be delayed for so long. Even with the drain on resources, it seemed much longer than normal. It was detrimental to the case too, because the evidence they needed to move forward with this investigation was currently tied up in those results. Lowe made a mental note to chase it with Chief Howard when they got to the station. "Anything they needed" she had said, and they needed the results of the analysis.

'It is weird,' Lowe, having returned to her plain, unflattering suit, agreed.

They pulled up to a coffee shop on their way in. Lowe hopped out, closing the door behind her and ran into the shop. It was practically empty, so there was no queue. She ordered two standards, self-consciously making her own a decaf as she remembered the results of the test from the night before.

The barista handed her two cardboard cups with heat-protective sleeves and she moved along the counter to add milk and sugar to Hayes'. As she was stirring the sugar into his cup, the old clunky TV in the corner of the coffee shop caught her attention. She listened and watched as the news report on her apparently famous criminal aired.

The reporter provided narration over the images: "Here we see Doctor J. Warren checking into a hotel near the hospital he works at, following being brought in for questioning by police yesterday evening. Our sources tell us he met with his lawyers this morning to file for a divorce from his wife of nearly twenty years. This development comes after news broke of shocking allegations of sexual assault against the doctor in the case involving journalist Anna Miller. A situation which must be a devastating blow to one of the country's leading cardiologists as he is due to appear before an interview panel tomorrow, regarding a promotion to Head of Cardiology at Hammersmith..."

Lowe put the top back on the paper cup and rushed out of the shop. She got into the car, handed Hayes his coffee, and slammed the door shut, turning to her partner, impatient to share the news.

'She's divorcing him.'

'Who?' Hayes asked, not really paying attention as he took a sip of the coffee, which was so hot that he burnt the roof of his mouth and screwed up his face.

'Elizabeth Warren.'

'What? When did that happen?' he looked to Lowe surprised, already forgetting he had just burnt himself.

'It was on the news. Come on.'

'Right. On it.' Hayes placed his cup in the holder and pulled out, driving in the direction of the Warren house. He was glad his partner was back to being focused. He knew this would help.

As they arrived outside the black door of number twenty-nine, Hayes switched off the engine and took another sip from his coffee, which had now cooled to drinking temperature. Lowe had barely touched hers.

'Uh, just remember, she's been through a lot in the last few weeks and she's not your biggest fan. Go easy,' Hayes advised Lowe as they walked up the steps to knock. Theo opened the door.

'Oh, hello lad, we're...' Hayes began.

'I know who you are. Mum's through there,' he stood aside to let them in and indicated to the living room. The detectives walked through, noticing the house wasn't as pristinely clean as it had been the first time they'd visited to attend the crime scene. Elizabeth was in the adjoining kitchen, washing up bowls from the morning's breakfast.

'Elizabeth…' Lowe called her, finding it fit to use her first name in light of the news of a divorce. Elizabeth looked up to see Lowe and Hayes, Theo standing beside them.

'What do you want Detectives?'

'Uh… we wanted to check in and see if you were OK?' Hayes tried to read her blank face.

'Yes. I'm fine,' she took off her yellow washing up gloves and came to the front of the island counter. 'Was there something you needed?'

'Maybe we can sit and talk?' Hayes gave a hopeful look.

Elizabeth held out her arms, motioning for them to sit on the plain fabric sofas behind them. They took a seat, and she joined them sitting in the armchair, which looked as though it was there more for décor than function.

'Would you mind giving us a moment, Theo is it?' Hayes nodded to him. He looked to his mother warily.

'It's OK Theo, go and check on Grace,' she reassured him. He left them to it.

'He's a good'n!' Hayes complimented.

'He is,' Elizabeth smiled thoughtfully.

'Is your daughter OK?' Lowe asked unexpectedly. Elizabeth's brows dipped in confusion. Lowe motioned to the ceiling awkwardly. She was trying hard to be nice and mend bridges. 'Grace, that's your daughter, you asked him to check on her…'

'As you can imagine, it's been a rough few weeks, especially for Grace, what with everything in the media, online and also here at home,' Elizabeth explained.

'I'm sorry,' Lowe said sincerely. In truth she was apologising for so much more than asking a stupid question. She believed that ultimately, she was the one responsible for the destruction of Elizabeth's family. In truth, it had very little to do with her.

In fact, Lowe's investigation had finally given Elizabeth the opportunity she needed to move on, although she would not reveal this to them. She still wasn't ready for the world to know what Joseph did to her, and even if she was, she couldn't release it anyway. She couldn't do that to her children. Joseph was, after all, still their father.

'So why are you here?' Elizabeth asked.

'We want to let you know what's going on in the investigation. I think we owe you an explanation, given the media frenzy,' Lowe explained. Elizabeth pursed her lips. She didn't want to hear it. She already knew, probably more so than the detectives. Lowe shuffled forward uncomfortably on the couch.

'Anna Miller – the woman we found in the bedroom downstairs – she woke up. She offered a different account of what happened, which suggested that your husband is the person responsible for Ed Braithwaite's death...'

Lowe waited for Elizabeth to respond. She didn't. Not even with a non-verbal expression. This was an abnormal reaction to the news. Most people were at least visibly shocked. Elizabeth was not. She simply looked at the detective and waited, so Lowe went on.

'...Uh, there was also suggestion that your husband did sexually assault her. I'm sorry to have to tell you this.'

There was a long pause. Lowe's stomach churning broke the silence. She rubbed it, feeling the sickness rising within her from drinking just the one sip of coffee, which it turned out she didn't like anymore. She smiled apologetically as she stifled it.

'Thank you...' Elizabeth offered, after watching Lowe closely and realising she was supposed to react, '...for telling me.'

'We can get a specialist officer in, to help you process all this, help the kids,' Hayes informed her. She smiled at him, but her attention was still drawn to Lowe. She seemed much calmer than the previous encounters, but less in control. She looked exhausted and she was trying hard to be nice. She needed something.

'There's more, isn't there?' Elizabeth raised her eyebrows.

'Yes,' Lowe told her honestly. 'At the moment, all we have is Anna Miller's words against your husband's. Now, we're quite sure she is telling the truth, but the problem is we need something more solid to make an arrest. It seemed to me – and again, I apologise for putting this so indelicately – given that you are divorcing him, that you might know something that we don't. You might be able to help us?'

Ah. There it was, thought Elizabeth. Lowe looked at her hopefully.

'Don't you have any forensic evidence?'

'It's a long process,' she screwed up her face.

'We were hoping you'd be open to helping us in the meantime?' Hayes tried.

'I don't understand what it is you want from me,' Elizabeth lied.

She knew she could help, but she wasn't sure she was ready to put it out in the open. She wasn't ready for her children to be dragged into the repercussions of the man their father was. She couldn't risk it being released all over the media. She and her children still had to go out in the world and face people too. What's more, if she handed over the camera, she was handing over her security blanket. It was her leverage for keeping herself safe. Her way of protecting her children from the people that would blame them for their father's actions. Can you imagine what they'd say about the woman who married the famous murderer and rapist, let alone to the child of one?

'Just, if there is anything, anything at all, that you saw, heard, or know that could help us, we'd really like to know,' Hayes clarified.

'There isn't.'

'What about the charge twenty years ago, do you know anything about that?'

'I told you, I don't know anything about that.' Except that she did. She knew exactly what it was and exactly why it was dropped.

'You didn't actually say...' Lowe pointed out.

'Well, I don't,' Elizabeth snapped. She wasn't ready to talk about it, no matter how hard they pushed. She'd tried to talk about it when it happened nineteen years ago, but she'd been shot down by two similarly dressed detectives, who had told her that it was her own fault for getting drunk. She wasn't about to let that happen again. Not after she'd finally found the courage to stop blaming herself, stop letting him control her and stand up for herself.

'Alright.' Hayes said, bringing it in. 'We don't need to know right now but if you do think of anything, anything at all. Please.'

'Help us. If not for us, for your friend Ed. And if not for him...' Lowe sighed, standing up ready to leave, '...please for Anna Miller.'

'For Anna Miller?' Elizabeth was taken aback.

'You have a daughter. She's someone's little girl too.' Lowe wanted her to feel emotionally responsible. She was sure Elizabeth could be the key to helping them.

Elizabeth sank into her chair. She hadn't given much thought to the woman her husband had hurt. She'd been so focused on her own anger towards her husband and securing freedom from him, that it hadn't really crossed her mind that there was another woman out there, feeling the fresh raw fear that she'd felt all those years ago, when he'd done the same to her.

Elizabeth swallowed but remained reticent.

'For the kids. They'll help.' Lowe set down a card on the table in front of her. It was a business card.

Elizabeth looked up to meet Lowe's eye. Something was different. The detective had treated her children and feelings with such disregard before, that it seemed weird to Elizabeth that she would suddenly be concerned about their wellbeing. Why would she suddenly seem to empathise with her as a mother, unless… oh!

'You're pregnant,' Elizabeth blurted out, without thinking. Of course, that made sense. The signs were all there. Lowe's pantsuit was a little too tight when they'd first met. She had always seemed irrationally snappy and short, likely courtesy of additional hormones. She looked tired. She'd been feeling sick right there in the living room. Even without those signs, Elizabeth was sure she could sense it.

Hayes shot a surprised look to Lowe, who stood staring, horrified. What kind of detective was he if he hadn't even picked up on that? Now he thought about it too, it was obvious. Her short temper had been unusual: she was usually fairly patient. More obviously the fact that she kept throwing up in her mouth, like from the smell of the corpse; he'd never seen that bother her before. How had he missed the fact that her clothes were getting tighter, that she'd stopped drinking coffee, that she'd instinctively been touching and protecting her stomach without realising.

Lowe cleared her throat. 'Thank you for your time Mrs…uh, Elizabeth. I think we're done here for now, but if you do think of anything, please give us a call.'

Elizabeth took the hint, stood up and showed them to the door. They began to walk down the few steps but before they got to the bottom, she called out to them, something compelling her to offer Lowe a little bit of help.

'You're waiting on forensics?'

'Yeah?' both detectives turned.

'Only his friends call him Joe,' Elizabeth riddled before closing the door, leaving them in a state of confusion on her doorstep.

The Forensics

Back in the car, Lowe tried to figure out what Elizabeth's cryptic sentence had meant. In the driver's seat, Hayes was more concerned with a different riddle – his partner, and he was trying to figure out the best way to broach the subject with her.

'So... is that why you almost threw up in the bar?' he asked cautiously, his attention skimming between her and the road.

'What?'

'Well, are you?'

Lowe blinked at him blankly. Her mind was solely on the case and lost as to his context. 'Am I what?'

'Uh...expecting?'

'Oh. Yes,' she confirmed simply. He wasn't sure whether he was supposed to congratulate her or not. She wasn't offering him much.

'When?'

'I took the test last night,' she stated.

He paused for a moment of thought. 'Is it Rob's?'

Lowe's head shot in Hayes' direction, suddenly engaged with the conversation. How the hell did he know about Rob? She'd certainly never told him. Sure, Hayes had been at the bar when they met, but he hadn't spoken to or met Rob. She was sure no one had seen her leave with him. Besides, that was two years ago. She'd never spoken about Rob to anyone.

'How'd you…'

'What? Like I was going to let you leave a bar with a stranger without running a background check on him,' Hayes enlightened her, not even sorry. She huffed, not sure whether to be impressed or mad at him.

'Is that why you didn't show up for work this morning?' he flicked his eyes in her direction quickly, putting them straight back on the road.

'I don't want to talk about it.'

'Does he know? Have you told him?'

'Can we just drop it?'

'But Abs, a baby?'

'Not now Ellis!' she stressed. She wasn't ready to talk about it yet. She didn't know what to say, think, or feel. She had no idea what she was going to do. Hayes glanced at her again. She looked oddly vulnerable, suppressing her emotions in his passenger seat. He knew her well enough to know that he shouldn't push her. He would let her come to him when she felt the time was right.

'He came up clean you know,' he informed her after a moment, hoping it would at least help for now. She said nothing. Yet, underneath a small part of her was grateful to know that Rob's background was normal, and she had nothing to be afraid of. Too bad he'd moved on already, she thought.

Hayes dropped the subject, or at least out loud he did. Internally he remained concerned for Lowe and kept shooting glances in her direction as they made their way to the forensics lab.

***

They hadn't quite figured out what Elizabeth had meant yet, but they knew it had something to do with forensics and quite frankly, they were done waiting. Walking authoritatively through the sterile rooms, Lowe and Hayes made their way to the unit they needed, their black suits strongly distinguishing them against the pale lab coats. Finally, after a white maze of corridors, they reached their destination. Without knocking, they entered.

The room was average sized and full of desks that were littered with microscopes, scanners and computers. Cupboards lined the room, full of petri-dishes, and different specimens crushed into glass slides were mounted on the walls in frames. Most of the benches were empty and clean, except the one against the wall, where files and books were piled in neat little towers in the corner. The world of science was alien to the detectives. The most interaction they had with it was through documents and emails. Electronic communications from elusive strangers, whose results they trusted without a doubt.

'What can I do for you Detectives?' a skeletal man asked them as they approached the bench he was at. He said this without taking his eye away from the microscope he was looking through.

'Hi to you too Seb,' Lowe drummed her fingers on the desk, waiting for him to pay attention. He looked up to heaven and angled his chair to face them.

'I'm busy Lowe.'

'So are we. I need you to fast track a case for me,' she demanded. Seb grimaced. As if he didn't have enough to do. His team were already stretched as it was, and he didn't like having his day interrupted. He'd deliberately found a job where he didn't have to deal with people often, so he didn't appreciate it when detectives came down to the labs to pressure him. The problem was, he couldn't say no to Lowe. She was a Detective Chief Inspector. If she needed something badly enough to personally take the time to visit, it meant that it genuinely was important, so he would give her what she needed. That, and the woman genuinely terrified him.

'What's the case?' he sighed, pushing himself back from the desk, so he could wheel himself to the stack of files at the other end of the desk.

'It's the Doctor J. Warren case. Number zero, six, eleven, eighteen,' she watched as he scanned across the tabs of the yellow paper files.

'Warren... Warren... Warren...was that a Joseph or a James on the first name there?'

'Joseph,' Lowe said, realising that if someone knew Warren, it wasn't Seb. She didn't know why she'd suspected him in the first place. Doctors. Labs. The connection just logically made sense, but it wasn't him. Seb was unsociable, he barely made effort with other humans and hated any attention being drawn to himself. It was unlikely he'd choose a friend that loved being the centre of attention.

Seb pulled out a file, pushing his small glasses up on his protruding nose to read. He mused over it. Closing the file, he looked up to them bemused.

'You should already have all the findings from us,' he said simply, now confused further as to why he was being chased.

'Wait what?'

'Yeah...' Seb opened the file to double check. 'Says here all the reports were compiled and sent over um, four days ago, that was within schedule. Signed and received by Superintendent Mark–'

'Tabbot,' Lowe finished under her breath. 'Oh my God,' she put her hand to her forehead and rushed out of the room.

Seb looked to Hayes, realising he had just put his foot in something much bigger than himself.

'Uh, thanks…thank you,' Hayes nodded awkwardly, going after his partner. Seb shrugged and continued on with his work. Whatever they had realised, it didn't concern him.

***

'What's Tabbot got to do with it?' Hayes caught up with Lowe in the large glass lobby.

'Joe.' She turned to him, everything suddenly falling into place. 'His wife, she said his friends call him Joe, right?'

'Yeah.'

'Well, yesterday when Tabbot called me into his office, he was having a go, he referred to him as Joe. Not Joseph. Not Warren. Not Doctor J. Warren like the press or on the case files. No, he said Joe. "You can't keep harassing Joe". That's what he said. Tabbot must know him and well, enough for Warren's wife to know who he is. That's why we don't have the evidence. You said it yourself, it's weird we didn't have anything. It's not weird if it's not late. It's been kept. He must have it. It all makes sense,' she spoke fast and fervently.

'But why would he? I mean, that's against the law…'

'Come on Hayes, he wouldn't be the first bent copper. Think. Right at the start, he forced us to assume Warren was innocent, he said it was a favourable narrative. He sent us off on random house calls to waste time, he wouldn't accept that Warren might be guilty? Why? Why was he so adamant he wasn't guilty? Why did he keep throwing us off that track? He's been so focused on Warren's appearance in the media. He keeps saying we need hard solid evidence. Ellis, he cancelled the rape kit!'

'Well fuck.'

'And he's withholding the lab reports, you know what that means?'

'Forensics say Warren's guilty.'

'He's covering for him.'

'But why? I mean why go to all that trouble, what's the connection?'

'I don't know...' Lowe walked around on the spot, trying to think, '...but I'm gonna find out.'

The Connection

The detectives were up against the clock now. They needed to find the connection before Tabbot destroyed the evidence. They needed to prove he was somehow involved in manipulating and intervening with the case to cover for Joseph and most of all, they needed those results.

He'd had the results for four days already – which meant he could have already started. It wouldn't be hard for him, with his rank, to take out evidence that condemned Warren and tamper with it. Have it retested by the lawyer to prove the original results wrong and get him off if it ever came to trial. No one would suspect him.

They devised a plan as Hayes drove back to the station, slightly over the speed limit.

'The results must be in his office. He wouldn't risk taking them home, not with his wife there,' Hayes mused.

'We need to find a way to distract him to get him out of his office,' Lowe agreed.

'And we need something to tie him to Warren.'

'Yeah. Phone records, emails, anything.' She knew there had to be something, but with little to go on, they were going to have to search through everything – even if it ended up taking all night.

Tabbot was preventing her from securing justice for Anna. He was preventing a criminal from being prosecuted. He was perverting the course of justice, and Lowe was going to take him down. Whatever the link was, she would find it, and he would pay.

'Would be great if we could catch them in the act,' Hayes fantasised.

'We'll try and check his phone, to see if they've been in contact,' Lowe said, assuming it a possibility.

'How are we going to do that?'

'You could stall him in the men's room...' she bit her lip. She needed a better idea than that, but the truth was Tabbot rarely got up from his desk unless he had a meeting. When he had a meeting, he locked his door. They'd either have to steal his key and wait for him to go to a meeting or they'd have to stall him when he left naturally to use the bathroom or go to the staff kitchen.

'How am I gonna do that?'

'I don't know. Tell him you think you have a growth or something and you're concerned.'

'I don't know what it is you do in the bathroom, but I am not going to ask Tabbot to check my balls,' Hayes looked to her horrified.

'Well I don't know Hayes, you have a better idea?'

'I'll figure something out, but yeah, I can stall him.'

'Good. Thank you.'

'Right, so I'll distract him, then you'll go in. Check the phone first, see if there is anything on there. Then look for the results. We need to prove he withheld the results.'

'We'll have to check the records when he isn't in. After work. You up for a late one?'

'I'll have Molly bring us some dinner,' he smiled, agreeing.

'No, don't trouble her. You're leaving her at home with your boys again... give her a break.'

'Please, I tell her you're pregnant, she'll bring us a bloody feast.'

Lowe wanted to argue with him, begrudging him for the reminder of the human growing inside of her, but she hadn't eaten a proper meal in days. 'Actually, that'd be great, I'm starving,' she confessed.

Hayes had already guessed that. He and his wife had two young sons of their own and so he knew the importance of ensuring a pregnant person was fed, and he knew Lowe was bad at remembering to eat.

'I'll let her know,' Hayes said as they pulled into the station. They were ready to execute the first part of their plan.

It was one o'clock so most of their colleagues would be out to lunch, and what few remained in the office probably wouldn't notice Lowe sneaking into the superintendent's office, though she'd have to be careful. As they had anticipated, the bullpen was practically empty, and no one was within eyeshot of Tabbot's office.

Both Hayes and Lowe sat at their desks pretending to do work and look busy, all the while keeping watch of Tabbot's office. This could work if he just left.

They waited.

Finally, he emerged, mug in hand. He closed the door behind him and walked in the direction of the kitchen.

'Action,' Lowe muttered to Hayes. He nodded and stood up coolly, following Tabbot. Lowe waited for the area to be clear, before looking cautiously around the room and going over to his office. Taking one last look behind her, she went it, closing the door. No one could see her now. She was safe.

She rushed to his desk knowing she wouldn't have long. She wiggled the mouse to see if the computer was still on. It was locked. She scanned the desk. His phone was still there. Bad decision on his part, to leave it lying about. She grabbed it. It was locked too. She'd never have time to figure out the four-digit passcode. She put it back down and looked through the drawers. Nothing in the top one. Nothing in the middle. Then, there, right on the top in the bottom drawer was a file. She opened it, knowing exactly what she'd find. The results. They were there. He did have them. She looked up, checking the coast was clear, before flicking through.

Over in the kitchen, Hayes had succeeded in distracting Tabbot. They were waiting for the kettle to boil.

'I wanted to talk to you actually Sir…'

'Oh?' Tabbot cocked a brow, still watching the kettle. He wasn't remotely interested. He just wanted his cup of strong black coffee.

'It's about Detective Chief Inspector Abigail Lowe…'

'Go on.' Tabbot turned, suddenly intrigued.

'I think, I don't know if you've noticed, but something seems off with her. Something is really distracting her from the case. I'm finding it difficult,' Hayes improvised, not really sure where he was going with it.

'Yes. I had words with her yesterday,' Tabbot agreed, finding it less interesting than he had originally thought.

The kettle clicked. It had finished boiling. He poured hot water into his mug over dry-roasted, instant coffee granules and stirred.

'Would you like one DI Hayes?'

'Oh no,' Hayes said without thinking. Tabbot placed the kettle back on the holder and picked up his cup to walk out.

Hayes blocked his path. 'Actually, I will have one I think.'

'Well, the kettle's just boiled Ellis, make one yourself. I'm busy,' Tabbot snuffed him, passing through the door of the kitchen, heading back to his office. Hayes followed him and noticed Lowe wasn't back at her desk. He tried to stall, but Tabbot kept on walking.

'So, Sir, about DCI Lowe... I was wondering if we could talk more about that.'

'Sure, we can do that in my office.'

'But...'

Inside the office, Lowe was still flicking through the file in the bottom drawer. As she was, Tabbot's phone buzzed. She looked up and pressed it. A message from a private number showed up on the home screen. She read the notification.

"Embankment. 6PM. I have the money."

Suddenly, voices outside. She looked up. Through the small frosted window on the door, she could see a figure standing outside.

The handle moved down.

Her eyes spread with panic. She put down the phone and thrust the file back into the drawer. As she was closing it, Tabbot entered, with Hayes behind him.

He jumped, startled to see Lowe standing in his office and nearly spilt his coffee down him.

'Lowe, what the hell are you doing in here?' He looked to her, waiting for an explanation.

'Uh...' she stammered.

'Well?'

'I wanted to talk to you,' she thought quickly, much better on the spot than her partner. 'Yesterday, you said I was distracted on the case. You were right. I am. There is a reason.'

'Right. Let's have it then. What's the reason?' Tabbot waited.

'I... Uh...' she blinked, ashamed of herself for the excuse she was about to use. 'I'm pregnant, and I'm sorry it interfered with my work. I won't let it happen again.'

Hayes looked to her from behind the superintendent, almost proud of her quick thinking. Tabbot blinked, stunned.

'Well, congratulations Abbie,' he said finally, going in and sitting down at his desk. She moved out, ready to make her exit.

'Thanks. I just thought as my direct superior, I should let you know,' she smiled awkwardly, backing out of the office.

'Yes,' he nodded, 'I'll get the forms from HR.'

'Great, thank you Sir,' she smiled. He looked to his phone and then darted a look up to the detectives.

'Close the door on your way out.'

They did.

Both took a deep breath. That had been a close call, but they had succeeded so far.

It wasn't over yet.

'Find anything?' Hayes asked quietly when they were back at their desks.

'He's got the results. I didn't get a good look at what was inside. And he got a text, private number. Embankment, six today. Something about money. I'm going to follow him. If it's about money, I need you to find the trail. I'll find out who he's meeting. We'll have enough to go to Chief in the morning.'

The Payoff

Five-forty came around. It was time. Lowe was ready. She watched, waiting for Tabbot to make his first move. The station was close. She'd have to keep a comfortable distance, but it would be easy so long as he didn't look behind him, although even then, she wouldn't be overly noticeable. She was dressed like so many other Londoners suited for corporate jobs, who would all be exiting with haste at this time of day. She would easily blend in with the wave of black, blue, white and grey.

Tabbot would have no reason to suspect he was being followed. Lowe guessed this wouldn't be the first time he'd done something shady, so he'd be experienced in covering his tracks. He certainly wouldn't assume that two lower level detectives, twenty years his junior, would figure it out.

He came out of his office in his jacket and locked the door. He waved a goodbye to an administrator near his office and exited through the double doors.

'Good luck,' Hayes wished Lowe as she got up, her jacket already on, prepared to follow Tabbot. She tapped Hayes on the shoulder indicating she was off, and left, following slowly and carefully behind the superintendent. She passed through the double doors, pausing and scanning the area. Down the corridor, Tabbot was stood, looking up and waiting for the lift. She moved forward through another set of doors to the stairs immediately opposite. She couldn't risk being seen.

As she reached the bottom, she stood peering through the glass panels in the doors, waiting for Tabbot to come out of the lift. He did. She watched him as he walked out into the small narrow car park, turning up the collar of his coat against the rain. She followed, leaving enough time so that she wouldn't be noticed.

Nothing but grey concrete and an assortment of cars separated them. She ducked behind Hayes' white Vauxhall, which was in dire need of a clean, and made her way along the row of cars, to the last one parked at the end. She kept an eye on Tabbot as he turned right, heading down towards the busy road that ran alongside the bank of the river. It was just a short walk down this A-road to the tube station.

Luckily, there were large trees on each side of the road for most of the path, which would make it easier for her to follow him. She did so, moving steadily from one tree to the next. He walked with purpose. He didn't look behind him. He had a meeting to get to, and he had to be on time.

Lowe followed him down Victoria Embankment, past the large white building that was seemingly never-ending and displayed more windows than anybody could care to count. It would just be a straight path. Or so she thought.

As Tabbot passed Horse Guards Avenue he veered left into Whitehall Gardens. Lowe kept eyes on him, following adjacent, still out on the pavement. Soon, bushes, trees and shrubberies clouded her view. She had lost sight of him. She thought quickly. It didn't matter, she knew where he was going. She rushed forward to the end of the gardens, hoping to catch him again at the crossroads.

Just as she was reaching the curved corner of the road, Tabbot emerged from the black iron gates of the gardens. She took an immediate step back, knocking into someone as she did.

Tabbot's head shot round as the stranger grunted angrily, but at that same moment the beeping on the pedestrian crossing sounded. Without getting a look he continued on, ever the impatient city man. He couldn't wait for the next green man. That would take too long. He couldn't be late.

The stranger looked to Lowe angrily. She apologised, but he walked off in a huff. She didn't care. She watched as Tabbot crossed the road, heading towards the bridge. The heavy swarm of traffic and pedestrians taking to the streets for the daily performance of London's greatest show: Rush Hour.

Leaving enough time, she crossed the road without waiting for the signal, looking out for cars. She followed him through the dark passage underneath the bridge, falling into step with the sea of workers around her.

The station was just on the other side of the Golden Jubilee Bridges. Tabbot had just minutes to spare. He turned left into the station. Lowe waited on the steps to the bridge, peering around the corner, watching. She couldn't see any one. She scanned over the shops, through to the other side of the station. No one looked suspicious, and Tabbot did not stop. Instead he turned left again, carried along by the wave of commuters.

He was going to the platform. She needed a ticket. She walked into the station and waited impatiently behind a woman who was taking her time to purchase a ticket from the machine. She was losing him. Hurry up, she wished, still observing Tabbot's movements.

Finally, the woman finished. Lowe quickly pressed the buttons, inserted her card and purchased a ticket but by the time she looked up Tabbot had turned off, heading towards the platforms.

She went through the machines and rushed after him. Members of the public eyed her doubtfully, her movements suspicious. Their judgements were irrelevant. She was so close. She couldn't lose him. She scanned faces as she travelled down the blue tiled tunnels. She couldn't see him. She looked more vigilantly. The turned-up collar stepping off the escalator.

There he was.

He turned left onto the platform. Reaching the bottom of the travelling stairs, she leaned against the wall. The long, curved platform was crowded, but she kept her eyes on her target at all times.

It was six. A train approached the platform.

A battle ensued as individuals tried desperately to cram into the carriages. Everyone moved forward in a determined bid to be victorious in conquering this train, even though another would be along in a few moments. Although by then, more people would have enrolled in the never-ending war of the underground.

There was one person however, who did not join the struggle.

He stood. Watching and waiting. Lowe stopped at the other end of the platform. If she wasn't careful, she'd easily be spotted. She sank back behind the corner, people passing her cautiously. She undoubtedly looked shifty, lurking there. She took out her phone and opened the camera app, switching it to front facing so she could see and record at the same time. She held it around the corner and angled the phone until she found Tabbot.

There he was. She peeked quickly at him standing on the platform as a man approached. She couldn't make him out. She zoomed in with her other hand, focusing on his face.

It wasn't Joseph.

She looked up disappointed, resting her head against the wall, but still recording. Then she remembered the face. She straightened up abruptly.

Joseph's lawyer.

Oh, that was clever. Naturally, he couldn't come himself. He was too recognisable. He had people to do his dirty work for him.

She watched the screen. They spoke, exchanging sentences inaudibly. The lawyer put his hand into his jacket and pulled something out of his pocket. Small, thin, white – an envelope. Tabbot took it, quickly stashing it into his own jacket. They shook hands as another tube approached the platform. The lawyer backed into the train, drowning into the blur of faces. It departed and was gone. After a moment, Tabbot began walking back towards the exit and back towards Lowe.

She snapped her arm back in and darted to the other side of the platform. Tabbot passed her going up towards the escalators, unaware that he had been followed and watched. She watched him leave before taking a deep breath.

It was confirmed. She needed to get back and tell Hayes what she'd found.

The Trail

By the time Lowe had exited Embankment tube station and made her way back to the office, the darkness had drawn in. Hayes was sat at his computer, furiously scanning through documents, consuming all possible information. A volcano of paper had erupted around him. He had been busy. Lowe approached, shaking off her wet jacket as she did.

'How'd it go?' he swivelled in his chair to face her, hopeful. She placed her phone down in front of him, showing him the video that she'd recorded. He watched the minutes of the exchange. 'That's the lawyer. That adds up,' he said excitedly.

'Yeah, what d'you find?' she asked, half-sitting on the desk.

'It was a payoff. People always forget how easy it is to follow the money.' Hayes wheeled and grabbed a list of accounts with a few lines highlighted and pushed them under Lowe's chin. She took them, examining as he explained.

'Tabbot has been receiving cheques from Joseph's lawyer. This is listed as "consultancy services" on the statements. He's received payments three times since the twenty-fourth. One here, one there and there. If we assume there was a cheque tonight in that envelope, that's a fourth. They can't do it electronically or from the firm's

189

accounts because it would be flagged immediately as conflict of interest, since he is involved on the case and it hasn't been closed. Besides that, someone would probably notice. So instead, this guy, the lawyer, is using his personal account.'

'So, what... Tabbot gets a payment in instalments, or every time he does something to help Warren?'

'I guess so. Every time money has come out of the lawyer's account, the same amount has been put in a day before. I traced the transfer back, guess where it came from?'

'Warren's account.'

'Warren's account, like we suspected,' Hayes said.

'Can we prove a link between them. Communication? Anything?'

Hayes grabbed another stack of paper. 'Phone records. Tabbot's been receiving a number of calls from disposable phones. Random numbers. Keeps changing, but they are always around the same date as the money is transferred.'

Lowe looked over the documents. Everything Hayes was saying was right. She couldn't believe how easy Tabbot had made it for them to catch him out. It was more astonishing, given his job, but then many people in the precinct thought he was losing it as he got older. It's why he did mostly desk-based investigating now. He wasn't fit for the field.

'But there's more. I checked for pings.' Hayes shifted the mouse to make his screen active again. On it there was a satellite view. 'Now I couldn't get anything that would hold up as evidence from the towers, and the phones were disconnected immediately after sending. They weren't registered sims either. However, I was able to trace where they were purchased. All from the same store, bulk bought on the same day, can you believe it? Look at where the store is!'

He pointed to the screen. Lowe stood up and looked over his shoulder at the map. There in plain view, no more than five minutes away from the Warren house. That was pretty compelling evidence. He'd done it. He'd found it. The link, the connection. Everything here supported the conspiracy. Tabbot was going down, and so was Joseph.

'And do you remember when we visited Warren that first time in the hospital? He had a cheap phone on the table. I remember because I thought it was odd, given how fancy the house was...'

'Oh my god. Hayes, you're a genius!' Lowe complimented him in amazement. He smiled briefly but he went on.

'But here's where it gets really interesting....' he looked up to her victoriously and turned the pages in Lowe's hand back to the front. What Hayes was about to say would shock her even more, just as it had him when he found it. It tied everything up in his mind.

'Look at the dates and where they coincide with our investigation. We know this payment was to cover up the evidence. That's four days ago, when Tabbot got the results...that's when we got the CCTV.' He pointed to it. Lowe nodded, taking it in. 'I imagine today's payment was for him covering when we pulled Warren in for questioning and for having a go at you, trying to put you off track again, make you think you were wrong. Anyway, the one that shook me is this one. Look at the date.'

Lowe looked. Surprise and confusion contorted her features at the sudden harrowing realisation that someone else was involved, someone she'd never seen coming. The transfer had occurred on the twenty-fifth. The same day they'd been called to the crime scene. The day that Joseph Warren had been unconscious.

'But... that would mean...' she gasped. Hayes placed the call log in front of her and pointed to an entry made to Tabbot's phone from a number she didn't recognise.

'That's Elizabeth Warren's number. She called him from the hospital, right after we'd interviewed her. He cancelled the kit on Anna Miller after that call.' He placed Elizabeth's call log next to Tabbot's to prove his statement.

'She knew,' Lowe hissed vehemently. 'How did she know?'

'I think I can answer that too,' Hayes replied, one eyebrow dipped. Lowe couldn't believe it. He'd been busy. Very busy. If they'd have found this earlier on, Joseph would be in prison already.

'It's not quite what you think,' Hayes warned. 'See, I thought about the charge, the one before, nineteen years ago. I wondered if that was how she knew. Maybe she'd helped out then, it wasn't long after that they were married, right?'

'Right...'

'So, I looked over it again and I did some digging.' Hayes turned back to the screen, clicked into a file and scrolled down. 'Look who had the case...'

Sure enough, there was Tabbot's signature scrawled onto the paper. Lowe shook her head. The bastard had done it before. Hayes pulled up another file.

'Same again. Now, the names might be redacted on the case file, but they aren't on the legal documents for some reason. My guess is, Tabbot wasn't authorised to change them. Look at who was involved, look at who the victim was.' Hayes moved aside so his partner could read clearly.

The print was clear. Tabbot and the lawyer were involved in the case. Joseph was being accused and Elizabeth Lewis was stated as the victim.

'Lewis was her maiden name,' Hayes declared, unnecessarily. Lowe had already put that together.

'Shit.' Lowe stood up, running her fingers through her hair. She hadn't realised that Elizabeth had been the first victim. She'd completely missed that. She'd just assumed that Elizabeth had been protecting her husband and children. She'd been so convincing in her role as the doting wife and mother. Lowe thought Elizabeth might know what her husband was but that she was in denial and didn't want the world knowing. She assumed Elizabeth was protecting Joseph out of her love for him. She hadn't considered even for a moment that Elizabeth may have been acting out of fear.

'Why on earth did she marry him?' Lowe tried to make sense of the extremely complicated situation.

'Well, that's where it gets truly horrific,' Hayes looked to her sadly. 'She fell pregnant. Maybe she got scared. She went to the University for help, hoping someone there would listen. Problem was…'

Hayes threw down an old photograph of a collection of people standing in lines outside a stately building. He pointed to a tall man in the middle, resembling Joseph.

'…Warren's father was vice-chancellor for the University. I'm thinking he must have pulled strings. He paid Tabbot to cover up for him then. There are older payments, from Warren's father's account. The dad died last year,' Hayes stroked his beard. 'It's just awful. All of the people that she could have gone to for help back then, they weren't there for her at all. They were all protecting him. The genius medical student. I can't imagine what that must have been like for her,' he mused.

'And I guess after the authorities dismissed it, how could she then go home and tell her parents. No wonder she wouldn't talk to us. All the support systems, all of them that were supposed to keep her safe, they failed her. They're corrupt. Sexist. Pampering to white male privilege yet again. It's wrong Hayes. It's fucking wrong!' Lowe exhaled harshly.

193

She thought back to when she herself had been a lost, helpless teenager with nowhere to turn to, no family for support, not sure how to get out of her situation. She was afraid of everything. She lost all control, so when anyone told her that it would be OK, that they would help, even if only to fulfil their own self-serving needs, she believed them. Lowe couldn't imagine the hurt that Elizabeth had lived with all those years. Sharing a bed with the man who raped her, whilst watching the child he forced into her grow up.

The very moment Elizabeth had found Anna on that bed, she must have known. She'd been through it. It was likely she also feared the repercussions of her husband's actions if she didn't help, especially after witnessing what he'd done to Ed Braithwaite. If she didn't repeat what had been done years before, she could have ended up a corpse too. And she knew just the man who would help her husband. She'd never forgotten him. That's how she'd have reached Tabbot.

Their case didn't have just two victims anymore; it had three.

'The system failed her Ellis. It fucking failed her,' Lowe looked at him indignantly, the anger edging into the corner of her eye. She suppressed it as the double doors of the office screeched open.

***

Hayes' wife waddled in, balancing Tupperware in her arms. The door banged shut behind her. She was a short woman, with vibrant red hair and olive skin and as always, she wore the warmest of smiles across her dimpled cheeks.

'Oops, sorry!' Molly said with regard to the slam. Hayes quickly got up and walked across the room to take the food off of her. She beamed at Lowe and with her arms now free, she rushed over to hug her. Lowe patted her awkwardly on the back, still uncomfortable with affectionate physical contact.

'I heard the news. How're you doing?' she looked at Lowe meaningfully, still holding on to her.

'I'm OK Molly. Thank you for dinner,' Lowe smiled, releasing herself.

'Oh no trouble at all babe, you need to look after yourself now. Both of you,' she shot a glance at her husband, who was already digging into the tubs. He looked up guiltily and smiled at her. She rolled her eyes. 'Men... am I right?'

'She loves me really,' Hayes muffled, his mouth full of food. Molly gave a false scowl, that contained more tenderness than disparagement.

'Do you know what you're going to do?' she focused her attention back to Lowe.

'Uh...'

'Not our business Moll.' Hayes walked over to his wife and put an adoring arm on her lower back. 'And thank you,' he kissed her lightly on the cheek. She smiled cutely.

Lowe went to the tubs herself and picked out one of Molly's infamous homemade caramelised onion and beef pastries. They were to die for.

'Oh, you'll never believe it, Ollie took his first steps today. Ethan thought it was wonderful, he thinks he can play now. I think I recorded it here...' Molly started, taking out her phone.

Hayes and his wife cooed over their children. They were the most normal and yet incredible couple she knew. They laughed together. They smiled together. They fought together. They simply loved each other.

Eating her pastry in the background, Lowe watched them fondly as they enjoyed footage of their son's first steps and chatted a little about this and that: the kids, nurseries, their parents. She even found herself letting out a silent laugh as Molly at last noticed the paperwork that had taken over the area and excused herself. Hayes showed her to the door and held it open for her. She walked through, turned to her husband and leaned in to kiss him. She pecked him, putting a caring hand to his beard and smiling before leaving. There was a warmth between them that the loneliest souls craved.

Lowe looked down sentimentally to her own growing stomach and, despite everything that had happened that day with the case, she could now only think of one person.

Rob.

The Evidence

The morning was dry, but the rain from the night before had left a lasting fresh smell. Pure, blinding white clouds hovered around the police station. Cutting beams of light flooded in through each window as the sun sliced through the density of the clouds. The seasons were beginning to change.

Inside, Lowe and Hayes were ready. Despite their late night, they were in early, eager to present their findings to Chief Howard. They were waiting outside her office, equipped to ambush her the moment she got in. They couldn't delay. It was imperative she knew about and acted on this today. Then they could obtain the forensics results from Tabbot.

Chief Howard arrived, striding down the corridor to her office, her heavy heeled boots sending clops echoing with each step as she neared. Her brows dipped in confusion when she saw Detectives Lowe and Hayes waiting for her, file in hand.

'Morning Detectives,' she greeted them with a nod and pulled out the small silver key for her office and stuck it in the lock.

'Morning Chief, we have something important to share with you,' Hayes gave her a firm look. She looked to Lowe, who stood with a similar fervent expression on her face. Chief Howard straightened her back and looked between her staff. Something was urgently wrong.

'Inside,' she instructed, pushing open the door and waiting for them to go in. They did. She followed, closing the door behind her. Neither sat, instead they stood hovering forebodingly. She put her briefcase down on the desk and stood opposite them, apprehensively awaiting their news.

'Right, out with it.' She put her hands on her hips.

'We've uncovered evidence that Superintendent Tabbot is interfering with the Doctor J. Warren case,' Lowe began.

'In what way?' Chief Howard asked, perplexed.

'We believe he's receiving payments from Joseph Warren to help him get away with murder and sexual assault,' Hayes explained.

Chief Howard's face sank. 'How'd you come about this?'

'We visited the lab. Seb said the results were sent to him five days ago now. He hadn't passed them on,' Lowe clarified.

'Evidence?' Chief Howard eyed the file Hayes was holding with anticipation. He handed it over to her as she pulled out the chair to sit. Then Chief Howard listened. She listened as they explained everything they'd uncovered.

They told her how Elizabeth had given them the tip, how they'd visited Seb, how Lowe had put it together, how they'd sneaked into Tabbot's office, which Chief Howard wasn't overly happy about, but understood in the wider scheme of things that it was necessary. They showed her the video Lowe had captured whilst following him, which she watched with astonishment. They told her how it hindered their investigation. She was already aware Tabbot had cancelled the SOEC kit at the hospital and had reprimanded him for it, but she'd put this down to an error in judgement. That wasn't what had happened at all.

They presented the trail of money, the call logs, the maps, the photos, the documents from the past case. They disclosed everything they had found, leaving little room for their findings to be disputed.

When Lowe and Hayes had finished and after viewing and hearing everything, Chief Howard leaned back in her chair, overwhelmed. It was a lot of information in one go. She put her hands together and rested her face on them thinking.

She thought of Tabbot, a colleague she'd known for nearly thirty years, who she believed was such a genuine, honest and good person. She thought of the temptation of personal wealth that he had succumbed to – not the first and likely not the last. She thought of how he had betrayed the trust of the force, his detectives and her.

She thought of the woman he had helped wrongfully indict. The woman who had suffered and would continue to suffer as a result of the tampered investigation. She thought of the backlash it would cause. The bad publicity. The difficulty from superiors. The internal investigation into the department. She pondered over the detriment Tabbot's conduct would bring and wondered what the best course of action was.

She looked up to the still standing detectives, who were waiting for her to say something. She realised how it had hindered their investigation, betrayed their responsibility, exasperated the burden of evidence for them. She knew they had done good work to uncover it and she knew she would have to act. But what should she do?

Tabbot had behaved wrongly. Unlawfully. She knew this, but she also knew him. He was a married man, with a wife and three children and two grandchildren. He had a mortgage, and a responsibility to them. Punishing him would punish his family. Was it fair to leave his wife with no money, no pension and nothing to depend on? Was it fair to Anna Miller to let him get away with it? How to choose between two evils…

'Alright,' Chief Howard exhaled finally. Lowe and Hayes held their breaths. 'Let's go get your evidence.' She stood up, scooping the paper back into folder they'd prepared for her.

The three of them marched through bland corridors towards their department. Chief Howard marched in through the double doors, her authority attracting the attention of the room as she did.

'Go back to your desks, both of you,' she ordered in a harsh commanding tone. They obliged but kept their eyes on Tabbot's office at all times. Chief Howard punched three hard knocks on his door and entered without waiting for permission. Tabbot spun on his chair clumsily, not expecting the intrusion. He stood up to greet his superior.

'Sit down Mark,' she spat bitterly, throwing the file under his nose. He could tell she was angry, but he wasn't sure why. He looked to her like a child in trouble – wide eyed and hoping he wouldn't be shouted at.

'W-what's this?' he stammered.

'Why don't you tell me?' She raised her eyebrows, placing two strong hands on her hips, lifting the sides of her suit jacket. She waited. He hesitated.

'Uh… I don't…'

'How could you?!' she interrupted fiercely, not being able to contain her frustration. He looked to her blankly and a little afraid.

'Michelle, I'm not sure what–'

'Don't you Michelle me. Now listen here you son of a bitch, you'd better have a goddamn good explanation for protecting that man against his crimes,' she pointed an angry finger of condemnation. Suddenly his ducks lined up in a row. She knew. She knew what he had done. He looked down, away from her disapproving glare. He'd never expected anyone to find out.

Outside in the bullpen, the busy flurry of activity came to an abrupt halt, all eyes shooting towards Tabbot's office as the shouts and yells of their Chief Superintendent hailed down on him with ferocity. They all exchanged looks with each other, unsure what it was about. Lowe and Hayes also exchanged glances, but theirs wasn't a look of puzzlement, it was a look of deep gratification.

Through the walls they could hear her thunderous questions shake fear into him again and again.

'What have you got to say for yourself? Do you understand what you've done? I should arrest you right now. Do you understand the implications your actions will have on this whole department? What were you thinking? Why? How could you?'

Each question triggered a subsequent rancid excuse from Tabbot.

'How could you?!' Again.

Then it all went quiet. Time floated around the still figures in the office, as clouds slithered across the sun outside, darkness shading the workers as they waited in trepidation.

Finally, Chief Howard emerged, slamming the door behind her. She scanned the room. An abundance of blinking eyes staring at her. She straightened her jacket and turned on her foot, walking over to Lowe and Hayes.

'Your evidence.' Of the two files in her hands, she handed them one. Lowe nodded a thank you, finally holding the results that she needed, that she'd waited for.

'What's gonna happen to him?' Hayes asked warily.

'We'll see DI Hayes. We'll see,' Chief Howard offered him an uncertain yet determined stare. With that, she left the room.

The staring meerkats in the office shifted towards Lowe and Hayes.

The Promotion

Within a minute, the nosy colleagues in the room had lost interest and returned to their own cases, the tension dissipating as the activity resumed. Tabbot remained ashamed and embarrassed in his office. He would not emerge for hours.

Lowe opened the file. She couldn't wait to read the report. Hayes watched her, interpreting her expressions at she read.

'We got him,' she looked up, a smile forming on her lips as she did, her face glowing with fulfilment. Hayes' mouth twitched into a reflection of hers. Finally, they really had him.

His fingerprints and DNA were tied to the murder weapon – the hammer. The blood on the hammer was a combination of both Ed Braithwaite's and Anna Miller's. It strongly implicated him as the murderer and attacker. Furthermore, the only place Joseph's blood had been found was on the bed and Anna's clothing, from where the scissors had pierced his stomach.

Ed's blood covered the majority of the findings. Blood spatter analysis concluded that he would have had heavy blows into the torso and head from a standing position near the foot of the bed from someone of a similar height, and that a trail of blood had leaked out, indicating he'd been pushed into the corner. The smeared handprints along the wall had been his own hands, covered in his own blood, as he fell backwards into that corner.

Nothing in the house suggested Anna had forced entry or let herself into number twenty-nine. The analysis showed that lots of tiny spots of her blood were found on the chest of drawers, wardrobe, floor and bed. Spatter direction suggested a blow to the head from the left whilst on the bed, consistent with Anna's now stitched up injury. They had everything they needed to arrest him for the murder of Ed Braithwaite and attack on Anna Miller.

There was only one disappointing finding from the results. They'd found no physical evidence to validate Anna's claim that Joseph had sexually assaulted her. This meant they could only arrest him on suspicion of sexual assault and Anna and her lawyer would be left with the burden of proof when it came to trial. Lowe had hoped she'd be able to find solid physical evidence to relieve the victim of this. She was saddened that she hadn't.

Her smiled evaporated. After everything, she would still have to let Anna down. If only Tabbot hadn't intervened. If only. Hayes noticed the change in Lowe's expression and was about to comment, when an administrator grabbed his attention.

'Sorry to interrupt Detective Inspector Hayes, there's a call on the tip line for the Doctor J. Warren case. Says he urgently needs to talk to the detectives working the case. Would you like me to put it through?'

'Yes, pop it through, thanks,' Hayes said turning to his desk and sitting forward, ready to grab the phone when the call was transferred to his extension. He didn't know who could be calling now... or why. Lowe looked up from the report and furrowed her brow. The administrator passed the caller through to Hayes' phone. It rang. He picked it up immediately.

'Hello, you're through to Detective Inspector Ellis Hayes...'

'There's something you need to know now about Joseph Warren,' an unfamiliar man's voice spoke in a hushed tone. Hayes stuck out his bottom lip and shook his head to Lowe as she looked to him inquisitively. He had no idea who was calling. He didn't recognise the voice.

'Who's calling?' he tried.

'I work with Warren. I want to remain anonymous. Who I am isn't important. I phoned in before, but there's something you need to know now. I'm trying to help. Trust me.'

'Right...' Hayes replied cautiously, 'What is it?'

'Warren's up for a promotion,' the caller said. Hayes screwed up his face. They already knew this.

'Yes, we're aware.'

'No. You don't understand. The committee are meeting with him today.'

Unsure where the conversation was leading, Hayes clicked his fingers and pointed to the pen pot, signalling for Lowe to grab him something to write with and on. She did so quickly. He moved the phone to rest between his shoulder and his ear as he listened to the caller. He wrote down "Warren. Promotion. Today?" for Lowe. She gave him a clueless headshake.

'He's not going to get it. They aren't going promote him because of all the accusations. It's too risky...'

Hayes crossed out the word "promotion" and shook his head slowly at Lowe without blinking, making sure she understood what was being said.

'...When he doesn't get what he wants, Warren gets angry. He'll be looking for someone to blame.'

Hayes wrote down "angry".

'Right, and why are you telling us this?' he asked, still unsure of the point of the call.

'Because though he generally works at Hammersmith, the panel is at Charing Cross; they're partnered under Imperial.' Hayes wrote this down for Lowe too. She wrinkled her nose, she wasn't following either.

'Yes,' Hayes replied blankly.

'Detective,' the caller urged, somewhat annoyed. 'Anna Miller is still at Charing Cross.'

Hayes' mouth dropped open. He turned to his partner, terror clouding over. Lowe clicked immediately.

'Shit!' She shot up from her chair, rushing out of the office, the report falling messily onto the desk.

'Hello?' the voice came down the receiver following the overly long pause.

'Uh, sorry. Thank you, thank you for calling us. Hold tight, we're on our way,' he assured the caller, standing, hanging up the phone and running out after Lowe.

They had to get to the hospital, and fast.

The Arrest

That same morning across the city, Joseph had been scrubbing up ready for his interview. Everything he had been working towards over the last decade was about to come to fruition. The long hours, the research papers, the charity work, including that godawful stint overseas, the extra shifts in A&E, the clinics at Charing Cross, the covering of staff holidays. All that extra work he'd done just to get noticed, all of it was for this – to become Head of Cardiology. He deserved it. He'd worked for it, and he was going to get it.

He fastened only the top button of his jacket, straightening it out and admiring himself in the long mirror, standing in the corner of the hotel room. He'd not been home since Elizabeth had asked him to leave. He couldn't have her handing over the evidence to the police, even with that money-grabbing idiot Tabbot covering for him on the inside. His lawyer had been to collect essential things: clothes, toothbrush, phone charger and so on.

He was still angry at Elizabeth for taking his children away from him, but he would find a way to get them back. She had no right. They were his. She wasn't financially stable, she couldn't provide the best life for them. He could, and he would get them back, by whatever means necessary. No woman was going to take away anything that belonged to him.

Right now, that would have to wait. It wasn't important today. Today he needed all of his energy for the interview panel. He smiled to himself. What was he thinking, all his energy? He was the most qualified for the job; he was going to get it. With one last narcissistic glance at himself, he walked out the door, prepared to start the next chapter of his life.

At the hospital, Joseph waited outside a room, sitting on an old chair. He was drumming his fingers on his knee and looking aimlessly down the corridor when the door opened, and he was invited in.

The room was standard, clinical, boring, and the furniture had been moved to suit the interview. Three chairs filled by three judges. Large long windows behind them cast in the cloudy morning light. A desk separated them from their interviewee. Joseph entered as if his audition for a talent show was about to begin.

He walked in and shook hands with all three, ensuring the widely approved firm handshake and then sat, poised, ready.

'Thanks for coming in, and thanks for waiting,' the man on the right started. He was old, lanky and balding. His smooth shining forehead reflective and tight in contrast to his rough wrinkling face. Silver glasses framed his beady grey eyes. His large, sloping nose and sharp chin gave him a stern authority.

'No problem at all, I'm excited to be here,' Joseph flashed them a charming smile, the kind that could so easily have lured anyone into a false sense of security.

'Well, I must say your CV is impeccable,' the man in charge complimented him with a copy in hand, looking up at the candidate through his glasses.

'I've worked hard. That's all you can do,' Joseph clasped his hands together.

'You understand this is a very important role that you're applying for here?' the second man, sat on the right, who was much shorter and fatter but only slightly younger, asked.

'I do. I think it would be a fantastic opportunity and a wonderful step up in my career. I think I would be a great fit for the role, I already know the team at Hammersmith and here, the ins and outs. I have the highest success rates and I look forward to driving a team to achieve the same,' Joseph boasted.

The woman in the middle shuffled uncomfortably in her chair.

'How would you intend to juggle your side projects if you were to assume the position... the radio and television shows?' the short man queried.

'This would be my number one priority. I would be one hundred percent committed to this job.'

'But you do intend to keep them up?' the woman asked for clarity, squinting in subtle disdain.

'I would, so long as they didn't interfere with my role here,' he replied.

'Doctor Warren, to be frank, we have some reservations about your public image and what it means for this hospital trust,' the spectacled man stated. Joseph began fiddling with his thumbs to suppress his growing irritation.

'You're talking about what's being going on in the news?'

'You understand, it already places this unit and this hospital trust in a compromising position, what with the current open investigation and the allegations–'

'Allegations. That is all they are,' Joseph stressed. The pressure was mounting. He was under scrutiny when he should have been under glowing review. Anna Miller was ruining everything for him.

She had already ruined his public image and his marriage, and now she was destroying his career. How could she? How dare she take everything from him?

'Still, they are very public allegations that have not yet been disproven by law. You must understand how it would look for the patients and shareholders of this hospital if we were to promote you right now…'

'What are you saying?' he looked at them in disbelief.

'The way we see it, Doctor Warren, is you've one of two options: you can either personally withdraw your candidacy from consideration, or we can formally decline your application.'

'No. No! This is ridiculous! I deserve this position. I have worked my arse off for it. You can't just disregard me based on some lies some bitch has sold to the papers!' Joseph stood up, losing his temper. They would not take this away from him. They couldn't.

'We really have no choice. Our hands are tied.' The old man crossed his fingers and closed his palms as if to signify he meant literally. He was unwavering. They all were. They simply watched as blood rose into Joseph's pale face like mercury in a thermometer. He huffed, looking between them, willing them to reconsider.

'I'm sorry,' the spectacled man said conclusively, standing up to hold out a respectful hand. Joseph glared at him, turned on his heel and marched out of the room, fists clenched. The fury boiled within him, his thoughts shrouded by anger, his view red.

Anna Miller was going to pay for what she had cost him.

***

The sirens wailed as Hayes meandered through traffic at an alarming speed. Lowe held on tightly in the passenger seat. It would have taken them roughly half an hour to get to Charing Cross

Hospital from the police station if they were driving normally, but that was too long. They needed to be there now. They needed to stop Joseph.

Lowe picked up the radio en route. 'This is DCI Lowe, requesting back up of one vehicle and arresting officers at Charing Cross Hospital, stat.'

Cars moved dutifully out of the way for the siren as the detectives raced against time across the city. Sixteen minutes later they arrived at the hospital, parking the car haphazardly outside. Slamming the car doors behind them, they ran inside.

***

Inside the hospital room that she was growing tired of, Anna was propped up in the bed, attempting to eat some ghastly hospital food. She was more comfortable now and had been freed of the many cables and tubes that formerly suffocated her. She'd been working with the wonderful team of doctors, nurses and physiotherapists, who had helped her manage to get out of bed and walk a few paces. She could now even take herself to the bathroom.

She was making excellent progress and if it continued, she would be able to leave in a week and continue her recovery at home. She was looking forward to this most of all, to seeing her parents properly, her friends, to being in the comfort of her own home, with a proper bed and shower. She also looked forward to reuniting with the family dog, a ruby cavalier spaniel named Whiskey. Most of all she was looking forward to being at home, in the warmth, the familiarity and the security it yielded. She wanted more than anything to feel safe again, and to rid herself of the nightmares that were haunting her sleep.

Anna turned her attention back to thoughts of Whiskey. His playful yet loving personality. His weird hatred of squirrels; whenever one was in the garden, he would bark at it incessantly. As she warmed herself with sentimental memories, she took another bite of something resembling a chicken curry. She was blissfully unaware of the danger that was charging towards her.

***

The detectives rushed into the elevator, apologising breathlessly as they took it over from visitors by flashing their badges. They pressed for the floor Anna was on and the lift took them up. They were so close.

***

But so was Joseph. Using his pass, he buzzed himself through onto the ward. He knew she was on here, but he needed to find out where exactly. He walked past two bays, searching for the woman he was after. The woman he was going to destroy. She wasn't there. Thinking on his feet, he pressed several of the emergency buttons to draw staff away from where he was headed, walking on as teams rushed to attend the patients.

Joseph approached the reception. He was going to charm the information out of them.

'Good morning. How are we today?' his teeth sparkled.

'Doctor Warren, you're back! How are you?'

'I'm doing fine. Just fine,' he lied. 'I'm wondering if you can tell me where a patient is... An, um... Miss Miller?'

The receptionists looked to each other.

'I'm sorry Doctor Warren, we can't do that,' was the wrong answer. His temper was triggered once more.

'I need you to tell me where Anna Miller is now, or I will have you fired!' he raised his voice.

Several bystanders stopped what they were doing as his tone become threatening. An alarm sounded. A flurry of staff came rushing to the central area. Joseph put his hand over the reception desk and grabbed the chart. The receptionist battled him, but the struggle was too much for her. She let go and all he needed was one look. He had his target. Straight down in front of him and to the left. Bingo.

***

The elevator opened. The detectives fell out into the lobby, skidding around the corner. They ran down the corridor towards the ward. Spectator's heads twisted around as they passed, many excited albeit confused by the racing action.

***

In her room, the sudden alarm startled Anna, just as it did many other patients. Curiously, she pushed the table of food away and swung her legs over the side of the bed. Slowly and with pain, she rose to her feet. She took hold of the silver stand, supporting the IV drip and wheeled it with her towards the windows of the room. She pulled apart the strips of the blinds to see what all the commotion was.

***

Joseph pushed people out of his way without care and went forward. He couldn't wait to get his hands around her neck, to forcibly drain the life from her. He would watch pitilessly as her eyes popped, begging him for mercy. He would have none. She had ruined everything. She should have died the first time.

Still peering through the blinds, Anna noticed the staff stumbling around after being pushed, a tall imposing figure emerging. Him.

She gasped, stumbling backwards. He was coming towards her. She was trapped. She couldn't run. There was only one door. She was helpless.

'Get back!' Sue yelled to Anna, darting into the room. Throwing the door shut, she pushed herself in front of it. Anna yanked the pole with her to the opposite corner and crouched down, closing her eyes.

Joseph reached the door. Sue tried desperately with the strength of her whole body to prevent him from entering but he was too strong. He overpowered her and barged into the room, knocking her off her feet.

'Get out of my way!' he bellowed. She clambered to her feet. Joseph grabbed her and threw her out into the corridor. He didn't care what damage he inflicted on the obstacles in scrubs. He could only see the woman he wanted.

Slower now, a dark sadistic smile lit up his face. Anna was cowering in the corner, her knees to her chest as she hugged them with both arms. Her eyes were closed but still leaked from fear.

'Please. Please. Please don't hurt me. Please. Someone please. Please help me. Please,' she was muttering pathetically under her breath, praying for help.

Joseph let out a menacing laugh as he bent towards her. Anna's eyes shot open to see those criminal blue eyes crawling into her vision. Her own wide eyes remained frozen in her shaking, broken body.

With one crooked, demonic smirk he grabbed her neck with his strong, steady hands and pulled her to her feet. He smashed her frail body against the wall, holding her there as she gulped for breath, just as he'd planned. He squeezed the air out of her lungs just as she had squeezed the control out of his life. Every time he tightened his grasp around her throat, he felt that control slithering back in. He had missed that feeling. He had craved it and now it was here, rising within him. He took one long sniff in, satisfied.

'No one's going to save you now,' he exhaled on her and kissed her forehead forcibly as she struggled.

Anna tried to pull his thick fingers away but was writhing so considerably for air she found she was unable. She could only look into the face of the beast that was killing her. A final tear dribbled down her cheek as he began to rinse out the last of her oxygen.

Joseph was about to unleash another maniacal snort as she took one last inhale, when a pair of large, strong hands grabbed and pulled him back, tearing him away from Anna, who crumbled down onto the floor. Joseph turned to see Hayes pulling him away from his target, Lowe right behind him.

They dragged him off of her, but Joseph resisted them. Hayes took the brunt of his force, pushing Lowe out of the way. Joseph may have been strong, but he couldn't defeat Hayes, who was not only robust but trained and prepared for physical combat. There was a scuffle as Hayes overpowered him and, in a final moment, twisted Joseph's arms behind his back. Lowe rushed forward, taking out two large silver rings joined in the middle by a chain – the symbol of human captivity.

'Joseph Warren, I'm arresting you for the murder of Edward Braithwaite and assault on Anna Miller. You do not have to say anything but, it may harm your defence if you do not mention, when questioned, something which you later rely on in court. Anything you do say may be given in evidence...' Lowe slammed the handcuffs around Joseph's wrist and Hayes ushered him out of the room to hand him over to the backup officers who were waiting in the corridor, aiding Sue to her feet.

Joseph Warren was done. They had him and this time he wasn't getting away.

'It's alright, it's alright, you're safe now. You're safe,' Lowe reassured Anna, who was choking and hyperventilating at the same time, as oxygen flushed into her lungs. Hayes rushed back in with nurses, who dipped to give Anna the essential medical care she needed.

Lowe got to her feet. She took one last look at Anna, panting on the floor as the nurses circled her and walked out of the room, Hayes following behind her.

In the corridor, she faced the criminal they'd finally caught. Joseph scowled at Lowe, saliva drooling from his mouth as he stood releasing feral huffs. Lowe narrowed her eyes, shooting pure contempt directly in his callous pupils.

'Put this animal in the zoo,' she instructed the uniformed officers. She would have nothing more to do with him. She and Hayes began to walk away down the corridor.

'This won't uphold Detective!' Joseph called after her, throwing one last gibe to the woman who would be the end of him.

Lowe stopped in her tracks. Slowly, she turned. Hayes stopped too, hoping she wouldn't react so heatedly as she had done in the past when he had provoked her. She shook her head simply, a determined glare sending a chill down his spine.

'Your time is up, Doctor.'

The Last Call

Lowe and Hayes walked out of the hospital to take a deep breath. Their case, aside from some basic admin, was over. They had done their jobs. They'd caught the bad guy. It hadn't been easy and there had been more to it than they ever could have imagined when they started out, but they'd finally reached it: the close.

As they emerged onto the busy street outside, they could hear the frenzy of press trying to get a comment from Joseph, the blinding phosphorescence of camera flashes sparkling for his last public appearance. Without pause, the two uniformed officers forced him into the back of a marked police car.

'Well, it's over,' Hayes said with finality.

'For us,' Lowe commented truthfully. They may have been done but the journey wasn't over for everyone. Not for Anna. Not for Elizabeth and not for the children.

'You OK?' Hayes asked, noticing his partner wasn't as happy as she should have been upon making the arrest and solving the case. Lowe's mouth scrunched up in one corner.

'There's one more person we need to tell it's over,' she remarked.

Hayes paused. 'The wife?'

'Yeah,' Lowe bit her lip. 'Hey, do you mind getting the tube back? I want to do it now.'

'Yeah, sure no problem. Keys.' He reached into his pocket and chucked her the car keys. She tapped him on the arm in gratitude and went to the vehicle, finding her way back to where it all started: the Warren house.

She ran up those horrible concrete steps for the last time and knocked on the black door of number twenty-nine. There was no answer. Lowe tried again. She heard a shuffling behind the door and the sound of the peep hole cover drop. She waited. The door didn't open.

'Elizabeth?' she called, knocking again. Someone was in there and if they hadn't answered the door it meant they didn't want to speak to her. It was Elizabeth. It had to be.

'Elizabeth, I know you're in there!' Lowe said, resting her head against the door and listening.

Elizabeth was stood the other side of the door. She didn't want to answer, she didn't want anything more to do with her husband or the police. She wanted to be rid of it all. She waited in silence, hoping Lowe would simply leave. She didn't.

'Alright, fine. You're not going to answer, but I want you to know Elizabeth, it's over. We know you helped him pay Mark Tabbot,' Lowe called.

Elizabeth edged away from the door slightly. She was in trouble. She'd only done that in fear that her husband would kill her, like he killed Eddy, if she'd tried to stop him or go against him. She couldn't let him do that. She couldn't, for her children's sake.

'I want to tell you it's alright. I know Elizabeth. I know what he did to you. All those years ago. I know it wasn't your fault. I know he hurt you,' Lowe spoke into the dark glossy door, hoping she would hear.

217

Elizabeth looked up with a subtle sense of triumph, but she remained unmoving in the hallway.

'It's done Elizabeth. We've arrested Joseph. He's in our custody. He's not going to walk free this time. He can't hurt you anymore!' Lowe listened closely through the door again for any sounds of movement. Nothing. She tried again, 'I just wanted you to know you're safe now. You and the kids.'

Lowe turned around and looked out onto the quiet, perfect street. Inside Elizabeth released a breath, the delicate hint of a smile forming.

'He tried to attack Anna Miller again,' Lowe said more softly, resting against the door. 'We got to him just in time. It's over for us – me and you now – so you can move on, forget about him.'

Outside Lowe realised she was saying the words as much to herself and she was Elizabeth. She needed to move on too, put the past behind her. She needed to start living. She picked herself up and walked away from number twenty-nine for the last time. She'd done what she came here to do, whether Elizabeth had registered it or not.

Elizabeth touched the inside of the door lightly with her hands, a strange melancholy passing through her.

***

When Lowe arrived back at the office, Hayes had made a start on the paperwork, ready to hand over to Chief Howard for the Crown Prosecution Service. She walked across the room to her partner and tapped him on the shoulder.

'How'd it go?' he asked.

'She wouldn't speak to me, but she heard alright. Listen Ellis, I need a favour please. Can you do something for me?' she asked determinedly.

'Yeah Abs, of course, anything. What do you need?'

'I need you to get me *my* file.'

'You're sure?'

'It's time.'

'You're really gonna tell him?'

Lowe had one last moment of doubt, but then she nodded with absolute conviction.

'Yeah. I am.'

'I'm glad.' Hayes smiled. Lowe was finally going to open up to the person she needed the most. She was going to let someone in. Most importantly, she was going to give herself a chance.

The Chance

Rob wasn't home when she got there. It didn't matter. She wasn't going to give up on this anymore. She'd made up her mind. She would wait. It would be worth it. His apartment was on the end, so she sat on the floor against the railings. With his front door on one side of her and the elevator doors on the other, it was as if she was sitting between the literal make or break of their relationship. One would lead to happiness. One would lead to loneliness.

It was dark outside and raining again. The ugly tiled floor was cold. Lowe sat in jeans and a black stretch top that showed the beginnings of a bulging bump. Rain drizzled in, wetting her hair, shoulders and back. Her casual, denim green jacket was folded over the satchel bag on the floor next to her, but she didn't care. She was so focused on thinking about what she was going to say, that she barely even noticed how cold and wet she was getting.

She'd only brought the bag to protect the paper file that Hayes had made up for her. It was relatively empty otherwise. Nothing else but her purse, keys, phone and the pregnancy test were inside. Lowe took out the test and toyed with it in her hands, fixating on the result as if the plus sign in the centre was the positive sign foreshadowing what was yet to come. Or so she hoped.

She hadn't ended things well with Rob. Time and time again, she'd used him and rejected him. She didn't deserve him. He was a good man. He'd even come up completely clean in Hayes' check, and Hayes was a thorough researcher. Rob had been honest and open about what he wanted. He'd let her hurt him, break him repeatedly – and for what? She didn't blame him for giving up on her. He'd been a fool not to do it sooner.

Lowe scrunched her knees into her chest and rested her head on them. It was late. Nearly ten o'clock. She didn't know where he was at this hour. Perhaps he was staying with that attractive woman she'd seen him with. Perhaps her coming here would all be for nothing.

The elevator dinged open. Rob, in his long black coat, stepped out of the lift, shaking off the rain. He walked straight past Lowe, across to his door, keys in hand. Lowe looked up at him, feeling more distant to him than ever before, her movement catching in his peripheral vision. He looked down to the drowned rat on the floor.

'Abbie? What are you doing here?!' His hands were still on the door handle. He didn't move. She was soaking wet and must have been freezing. She looked a sorry mess. Was she here to play games with him again? She probably just needed him, so she could take a break from her case. What was she expecting, him to be home and waiting for her? He wanted to be angry that she had shown up unannounced, but somehow found himself unable to be. Looking down on her like this, he felt a deep urge to scoop her up and make her warm. He resisted that urge. He knew where it got him.

'Hi,' she exhaled as she so often did, but something was different. It wasn't the normal expectant greeting. This one was loaded with apprehension.

'Why are you here?' he waited.

'We finished the Doctor J. Warren case...' she began to try and explain, offering a case report by default. Rob looked up to heaven, exhaling in frustration.

'Good for you Abs. Go home.' He turned his handle.

'I saw you,' she blurted out, desperate for him not to leave her there. He stopped. 'With that woman. You brought her here.' Lowe bit her lip, jealousy leaping into her eyes.

He let out a laugh, looked to his feet and shook his head. He didn't look at her. 'If that's why you're here, you... just go home Abigail.'

'Do you like her?' She found fighting with him so much easier than opening up to him, but he was too tired.

'That's not. You shouldn't be here. She isn't. She's no one,' he huffed and turned, finally meeting Lowe's eye, before finishing resolutely. 'No. I don't like her.'

'Oh.' Lowe wasn't sure how to go on, how to tell him.

'So, what are you doing here?'

'I needed...I wanted you,' she stuttered honestly. The words opened a wound in his heart.

'I told you, it's over. Get lost Lowe,' he told her angrily, opening his door to go in.

In panic, she threw the pregnancy test at him. It flew into the door and landed at his feet. He looked down, confused and stooped to pick it up. Lowe got to her feet to leave. She had done what she had come here to do – sort of.

Rob's eyes widened as he read the result. She passed him, bag over shoulder and jacket in hand, and pressed the elevator button.

'Where are you going?' he turned to her. She stopped and faced him.

'Uh, I don't...' she paused as he walked closer to her.

'Are you gonna keep it?' he asked, raising his eyebrows. He stopped opposite her. Lowe nodded her head, a single tear sliding out of her eye. He looked at her, for the first time seeing a side of her he hadn't seen before. She was scared. His face twisted in sympathetic pain. It killed him to see her almost crying.

'Is that all you came here for, to tell me?' he asked more softly. She looked away, afraid to meet his eye, frightened he would reject her now. She shook her head. He breathed and studied her. She didn't move, but waited, shivering on the spot, for him to say something.

The elevator door opened behind her.

'Fuck,' he exhaled warmly, giving in to himself. 'You're freezing...come on.' He took her hand and led her inside his apartment, where he offered her a warm jumper to change into.

Lowe changed in the bedroom area, and then took out the file from her bag. Returning much warmer and much drier, she walked across the apartment to find Rob in the lounge area, a neat bourbon in hand. He saw the file in her hand and met her eyes to question it. She went forward and sat next to him, placing it on the low, white glass table in front of him.

'What is it?' he asked, cocking a brow in her direction.

'It's why I've been a pain in the arse,' she told him humorously.

'Alright,' he took it hesitantly and opened the file.

'I'll make tea.' She got up, heading over towards the kitchen. She couldn't bear to see her history again. She already had it, every day, ingrained in the back of her mind.

As she boiled the kettle and made herself a cup of tea on his modern kitchen island, Rob read. And he saw. And he understood. He looked over every detail of the terrifying events that consumed Lowe's childhood. He learned of her father who walked away, leaving her to care for a younger sister whilst her drug-addicted mother gave up on life. He saw how they both were murdered, how the killer was never caught. He read everything.

He looked up, fighting back tears of his own. He'd had no idea. He couldn't even begin to fathom how someone could go on enduring life after that much pain and suffering. Yet, somehow, she had. Now everything about her made sense. Her reluctance. Her distance. Her lack of commitment. Her worry. It wasn't necessarily that she didn't love him, it was that she was afraid to. He could just as easily walk away, leave. Except, that wasn't who he was.

He wasn't the kind of man to walk away from the woman he loved and if he had to spend every hour of every day reassuring her that he wouldn't leave her and that he cared for and loved her, he would do that. He wasn't going to abandon her. He was going to be there. He got up and walked into the kitchen and there, gazing up at him, there she was.

He focused on her, walking forward, saying nothing. Lowe followed him with uncertain eyes. He reached her. His broad hands reaching out to cup her face. He kissed her, softly, on her lips. Her hands lifted to his waist, and then she relaxed into him. Her arms wrapped around him, her head sinking into his protective chest. She closed her eyes and found comfort. He kissed the top of her head, before resting his chin on it and hugging her right back.

They talked for a long time that night as she found faith in herself, enough to admit she loved him back, wanted to give their relationship a chance and importantly, wanted to keep the baby.

They were going to make it.

The Burden

There was just one thing left to do on the case and that was turn in the reports to Chief Howard, which Lowe (in the same outfit from the night before, her green jacket, blue jeans and black stretch top) was ready to do. She knocked on the door and entered. Chief Howard was sat at her desk, waiting for the file.

'Ah, thank you DCI Lowe.' The chief took the report. Lowe turned to leave, ready to take on whatever case she was assigned next.

'Uhm, you did good work on this.'

Lowe stopped in her tracks and gave a grateful smile.

'No really. You should be proud of yourself Abigail. And I'm sorry, that we didn't pick up on anything suspicious with Tabbot before. It was our failure. Warren will be going to trial I imagine. The murder and attack will stick. I have doubts about the sexual assault claims. But still, you did it, you got the right person. Well done.'

'What's going to happen to him?'

'Mark?' Chief Howard took a deep breath. 'We've somewhat forced him into early retirement.'

Lowe scoffed, struggling to withhold her contempt. Was that it? The man had broken the law. Everything she and Hayes had worked hard to uncover now meant nothing, nothing at all. Tabbot had perverted the course of justice, he'd tried to help a murderer and a rapist get away with it and had taken payment for those services. He was a dirty officer. A morally sick man.

'It was the best option, given everything. He has a family who depend on him. We have to consider the bigger picture.'

'No. Don't you get it? You're covering up what he did, just like he tried to cover up for Warren,' Lowe shot. She was angry. How could anyone actually think that was the rightful decision?

'He has his flaws, Detective,' Chief Howard said firmly, 'and he made his mistakes, but he's not a bad man. He doesn't deserve to go to prison. I've consulted with the Commissioners and this is our decision.'

Lowe looked to the ceiling in disbelief. She hated them. Those faceless upper-class suits, walking around as nothing more than an expensive paycheque, and Chief Howard was just as bad. Immoral. Corrupt. Self-serving. Working purely to uphold an internal political system and an outwards projection of a functional, working service. Doing the right thing didn't matter here. All that mattered was image.

'I wonder if a woman would have been extended the same mercy,' Lowe spat.

'It has nothing to do with that DCI Lowe,' Chief Howard argued.

'Really? Then where was your consideration for what was just for Anna Miller? Huh, what was the best option for her?'

'The circumstances are different,' Chief Howard defended pathetically. Lowe shook her head in disappointment.

Rightfully, Chief Howard should want to ease the weight on the victim who had already suffered, but instead she'd done what she could to protect a man who had broken the law, all because he had a family and some financial responsibilities, and probably because it would "look bad" for the service publicly.

Lowe turned, disgusted, and firmly asked her one final question.

'Why do we keep making excuses for men but expect explanations from women?'

It was the question any decent human should have asked. A question the system failed to ask. A question society failed to ask, and more disappointingly, failed to correct.

Chief Howard opened her mouth and closed it again like a fish. She had no answer. Lowe shook her head once more, disapproving of the chief, the system and society.

'I'm done,' she said resolutely. How could she serve in an organisation she believed was fundamentally flawed? 'I'll give DI Hayes my resignation.'

Lowe turned on her heel without giving Chief Howard the chance to respond and did just that. She went back to her computer, typed it up, printed it and put the piece of paper down in Hayes' hands, before striding out of the building.

Hayes read the letter of resignation and rushed outside to catch her.

'You're quitting?' he called after her in the car park. She turned.

'Yeah,' she called back. 'I'm sorry.'

Hayes scuttled over to her. 'Sorry for what? What are you going to do?'

She shrugged. 'I don't know Ellis, maybe I'll PI or join an agency. I really don't know, but I can't work here anymore.'

'What happened?'

'They offered Tabbot early retirement.'

'Aw, shit. Surely not, they can't have done that. Not after what he did. Surely they considered the effect his actions would have on Anna Miller?'

'Yeah, well they considered the effect it would have on Tabbot's life much more important.'

'You're kidding?'

'Such is the burden of being a woman.' Lowe shrugged downheartedly.

Hayes looked to his partner and friend meaningfully. She seemed different. She was exhausted of being trapped under the burden of fighting for justice in a hopeless and perpetually broken system. He knew then, looking at her, that she wasn't quitting. She was freeing herself. She could no longer be a cog in an archaic, backwards and damaging machine. She would start again, with something she could believe in and whatever she went on to do, Hayes was sure she would succeed.

'Well, I expect baby pictures. You know Molls will kill me if I don't get them,' Hayes smiled at her. She looked to him warmly. He truly was the kindest, most understanding man she'd ever met.

'I'll be at Rob's. I trust you know where to find me?' she smiled back.

Hayes walked forward and embraced Lowe. She hugged him back. A friendly, well-wishing goodbye. Though they would keep in touch and she would miss working with him – the one person that gave her faith – every day, she had to close the door on this part of her life now.

As she let go, taking in one last nostalgic look at the wonderful man she'd had the pleasure of serving beside for the last decade, Lowe realised there was just one last stop she had to make.

She got into her car and drove towards the hospital.

The Women

Lowe entered the boring square hospital room. Anna shifted her weight forward upon seeing the detective.

'Hi,' Lowe smiled, walking over to Anna.

'Hey.'

'How're you doing?'

'Better knowing he's behind bars,' she admitted. 'Thank you, by the way Detective. I never thanked you…for believing me.'

Lowe gave a woeful smile. 'I do believe you Anna. I still do, but that's why I'm here.'

Anna's face dropped as she looked to Lowe uncertainly. Lowe put a few business cards down on the table, which wasn't being used and so was positioned at the foot of the bed.

'It's not quite over for you yet. You'll need a lawyer. Those are some good ones on the cards. I'm afraid it's likely you'll have to relive it for them and possibly in front of a judge and jury in court–'

'Maybe she won't have to,' a voice interrupted from the doorway. Both women looked over to find a third standing timidly at the threshold in a beige trench coat, her handbag dangling from her fingers in front of her legs.

'Elizabeth?' Lowe didn't understand what she was doing here and was surprised to see her.

Anna looked between the two older women in the room. She'd never seen Elizabeth and had no idea who she was, but it was clear the detective knew her.

'Who is she? Who are you?'

'Anna, this is Elizabeth. She's...uh...Joseph Warren's wife. She's the one that found you,' Lowe informed her awkwardly.

Elizabeth swallowed and remained firmly at the threshold. She did not take a step further. She was afraid to. She felt guilty just by association as she finally looked into the broken eyes of the young woman whose life her husband had destroyed. She wanted more than anything to rewind the clock and ensure he was punished the first-time round, the time he had hurt her, but she had been too weak then. Too scared. Too easily manipulated by men in positions of power. She was here to make up for that.

'What is she doing here?' Anna asked Lowe intensely, before turning to Elizabeth with a sense of immediate dislike. 'I don't want to hear what you have to say. I don't want you to come in here and defend your husband. I don't care if he is married. I don't care if he has children. I don't care that he is famous. I don't care. It doesn't excuse what he did to me. And you should just leave...'

It seemed Anna was finding her strength, but she was taking it out on the wrong person. Lowe put her hand on Anna's arm to stop her. Elizabeth came a little closer but stopped as Anna shot her a warning glance.

'That's not why I'm here,' Elizabeth told her, nervously edging towards the foot of the bed. She stared into Anna's eyes, pleading to be given the chance to make up for her mistakes and to help. There was a long, weighted silence.

This was the first time all three women had been in the same room, yet all of their lives had changed as a result of one selfish, abusive and unforgivable man. Though it would impact them in different ways, change their lives separately, and their futures would be their own, they would forever remain connected and always remember the events that had happened inside the basement bedroom of that house with the black door and the glinting number twenty-nine above the paint-covered knocker.

'So, why are you here?' Lowe asked the imperative question.

Elizabeth reached into her handbag and pulled out the camera. One modern digital camera, the one Joseph had used to glorify his atrocious act. His trophy. She placed it slowly onto the bedside table in front of Anna and Lowe. Elizabeth had had it all along, but she had been unprepared to face the consequences of the footage on it.

Lowe knew immediately what this meant: proof.

To Anna, this camera began as a mystery that would ultimately secure her the justice she deserved.

Elizabeth looked to Anna, their part of the story just beginning as they bonded, sharing empathy with each other on an inconceivable level.

And then, with one final motion, Elizabeth pulled another chunky and dated black camera out of her bag and told Anna why she was there, finally saying aloud the words she had held in for so long.

'I'm here to say... me too.'

Printed in Great Britain
by Amazon